The
Perfect View

NICOLE PYLAND

The Perfect View

Tahoe Series Book #3

Adler Williams had been surprised with a trip to Jackson Hole, Wyoming, by her boyfriend; but not in a good way. That was the last place Adler ever wanted to be. She was not a woman who enjoyed camping or the outdoors in any way. While trying to return the camping supplies she wouldn't be needing for this surprise trip, she meets a woman who loves the outdoors so much, she runs an outfitter's shop in South Lake Tahoe.

Morgan Burns had watched her ex-girlfriend fall for and get engaged to her new girlfriend. Then, she'd watched her best friend get the girl of her dreams. When she visits Jackson Hole to plan a new store to her ever-growing chain, she meets a woman who is clearly not a fan of many of the activities Morgan holds dear.

The two women begin a long-distance friendship while they both attempt to navigate the newest hurdles in their lives: Adler's relationship with her boyfriend and Morgan's drive to expand her store empire. As Adler spends more and more time with Morgan, she begins to realize there's more to her life than just work; or at least there can be, as long as she's willing to risk her heart.

To contact the author or for any additional information visit: **https://nicolepyland.com**

BY THE AUTHOR

CHICAGO SERIES:

- Introduction – Fresh Start

- Book #1 – The Best Lines

- Book #2 – Just Tell Her

- Book #3 – Love Walked into The Lantern

- Series Finale – What Happened After

SAN FRANCISCO SERIES:

- Book #1 – Checking the Right Box

- Book #2 – Macon's Heart

- Book #3 – This Above All

- Series Finale – What Happened After

TAHOE SERIES:

- Book #1 – Keep Tahoe Blue

- Book #2 – Time of Day

- Book #3 – The Perfect View

- Book #4 – Begin Again

- Series Finale – What Happened After

BOSTON SERIES:

- Book #1 – Let Go

- Book #2 – The Right Fit

- Book #3 – All Good Plans

- Book #4 – Around the World

- Series Finale – What Happened After

SPORTS SERIES:

This series is related by a sports theme, not by characters.

- Book #1 – Always More

- Book #2 – A Shot at Gold

- Book #3 – The Unexpected Dream

- Book #4 – Finding a Keeper

CELEBRITIES SERIES:

- Book #1 – No After You

- Book #2 – All the Love Songs

- Book #3 – Midnight Tradition

- Book #4 – Path Forward

- Series Finale – What Happened After

HOLIDAY SERIES:

- Book #1 – The Writing on the Wall

- Book #2 – The Block Party

- Book #3 – The Fireworks

- Book #4 – The Sweet Escape

- Book #5 – The Misperception

- Book #6 – The Wait is Over

- Series Finale – What Happened After

ANTHOLOGY:

- The Meet Cute Café

FIRE UNIVERSE:

- The Fire

- The Disappeared

STAND-ALONE NOVELS:

- Reality Check

- The Show Must Go On

- Future Wife

YOUNG ADULT / NEW ADULT:

- The Moments

- Love Forged

- Pride Festival

EROTICA:

- Once a Month

CONTENTS

CHAPTER 1

"THIS is the last place I wanted to be," Adler argued. "When I said I thought we should take a vacation, I meant that I wanted to be sipping umbrella drinks on a white sandy beach somewhere." She waved her arm around with a flourish. "This is not a white sandy beach; and *this* is not an umbrella drink." She held out her canteen for emphasis.

"I know the iodine gives it a metallic taste, babe, but it's important to purify the water before you drink it," Brad replied.

"That's what you took away from my outburst?" she asked in disbelief. "That I'm mad my water tastes like it came from the river *and* like metal?"

"I thought I'd surprise you with a nice trip."

"This isn't a nice trip, Brad. A nice trip would have been a five-star beach resort." Adler capped her canteen, after not drinking from it, and tossed it onto the half-assembled tent. "I have to pee," she stated, standing at the same time.

"There's a good tree grouping over there." Brad pointed without looking up from the poles he was attempting to piece together.

"There aren't bathrooms?"

"Adler, we're in the middle of the wilderness. Where exactly did you think we'd be going to the bathroom?" He looked up at her, sweat covering his brow.

"You surprised me with this trip, Brad. You told me at the very last minute that we were going camping. Camping implies a campsite with at least the bare essentials, like an unsanitary but at least modern public bathroom."

1

"Well, there's toilet paper in my pack. Is that good enough?" he asked, sticking two poles together. "And I'm sorry I planned what I thought would be a fun vacation for us."

"I don't want to fight about this. I just want it to be over," Adler replied, rubbing her hands together for warmth. "And it's summer. Why is it so damn cold?"

"Are you going to complain the entire time we're here?" He tossed the connected poles to the ground in front of him. "This was supposed to be an anniversary trip where we reconnected, Adler. You haven't stopped complaining since we started our hike up here."

"When have you ever heard me say I want to go camping, Brad? Never. The answer is *never.*"

"I wanted to get you off your damn cell phone, Adler. I wanted you to stop thinking about work for five minutes. This was the best way I could think to do it. There's no cell reception here. It's just the two of us. We're in this beautiful national park, in a tent just big enough for both of us."

"And bear containers; don't forget about those. I read about that in the pamphlet they gave us when we entered," she replied.

"Fine. If I'm torturing you, we'll stay out here tonight – because it's too late to hike back to the road – but tomorrow, if you still want to leave, we'll hike down and I'll call a hotel from the car."

"Hotel, where?" she asked, hopeful.

"Jackson Hole. It's the nearest town. We drove through it to get here," he answered.

"It's Wyoming. It's probably the only town," she said. "I'm going to the bathroom."

"I'll get the tent up and start a fire for dinner," he replied.

"Can't wait," Adler said sarcastically.

She pulled the roll of toilet paper from his pack and walked through the group of trees he'd pointed out. She could hardly believe she was a thirty-five-year-old executive who normally lived in designer business suits and dresses for formal affairs when she squatted behind a tree. She finished, returned to the site, and watched Brad continue with the tent. She helped by pulling out the items they'd need to prepare their dinner. They moved around one another in silence for the next hour. The fire Brad had started was a small one, but it got the job done. She hadn't had ramen noodles since college. She hadn't missed them.

When she thought about how she'd thought they'd be spending their time together compared to how they were actually spending their vacation, she couldn't help but be disappointed. They'd been together for a year and a half. Brad had given her a two-week vacation as their one year anniversary gift. She'd been excited at the prospect then, but work had been busier than ever. She had to keep putting it off until finally, Brad put his foot down. He was about to start a new construction project back home in Seattle. He'd been awarded a massive government contract with the city that would keep him and his employees busy for the next several years. This was their last chance to take off before it started. She'd agreed to the trip, and also to it being a surprise, because it had seemed so important to him. She'd realized her mistake the moment he showed her their boarding passes with the Wyoming destination. She'd never heard of a resort in Wyoming. She was certain at least one existed, but when she'd thought about getting away from the hustle and bustle of her life back in the city, this was the last place she'd ever thought of.

They fell asleep facing away from one another in a cramped tent, with Brad snoring lightly behind her, as he always did when they shared a bed. Eighteen months in, and they still weren't living together – which was a problem according to her sister, Paxton; she thought they should have moved in together a long time ago. Adler, however, liked her space. Brad didn't seem to mind. As he snored, she listened to the sounds of nature around them. She hadn't taken the time to enjoy the view or the sounds of trees rustling in the wind, the crickets chirping, or the occasional howl from some animal off in the distance. It wasn't terrible. She turned her head back slightly as Brad shifted in his sleep, pushing her back a little against the thin material of the tent. She closed her eyes and decided to just make it through the night. Tomorrow, they'd pack, and she'd get checked into a hotel. She'd feel more in her element, and things would calm down. They'd have a much better anniversary trip once they had a plush bed and amenities.

***

"I'm going for a swim. I'll be back later," Brad told her a mere five minutes after they'd gotten to their room.

"Fine," Adler replied.

She felt bad. She knew he'd put a lot of time and planning into the camping trip, but not once since they'd known one another had he ever mentioned camping to her. Nor had she said it was anything she'd ever be interested in. Where he'd gotten the idea from, she had no idea. Because he'd failed to tell her exactly how to pack, preferring to arrange and bring everything they'd need for the outdoors himself, she'd packed for a real vacation. She opened her laptop bag – which she'd begrudgingly stowed in the rental SUV before they'd begun their hike the other day, then opened her computer, checked her email, and decided to do a little work while Brad swam.

"Are you kidding me?" he asked when he returned about an hour later.

"What?" She turned around to face him, noting the wet hair and towel he had slung over his bare shoulder.

"You're working?"

"I was checking a few emails while you went swimming. I thought we could grab some dinner when you got back."

"Adler, I asked you not to work while we're here. I get you for two weeks, and you're still working." He tossed the towel onto the still made bed and walked into the bathroom.

"Brad, I was waiting for you to get back. What was I supposed to do?"

She closed the laptop and stood, walking over to the bed where she picked up the soiled towel and hung it over the bathroom door.

"I'm going to shower. It's been a long few days."

"Then, dinner?" she asked.

"Then, I'm going to run the stuff I need to return back to the outdoor store," he replied. "Most of it wasn't used, and I still have the receipts."

"I can do that," she said.

"You're working," he replied, pulling the shower curtain back to start the water. "Want to join me?" He motioned to the bathtub. "We could shower together and then go to the store."

"I'll return the stuff," she answered. "I think we could both use a little space, anyway. I know I made you upset about the whole camping thing and just now with work. Let me at least return the stuff you bought to give me a nice vacation. I'll be back in an hour. We can go to dinner then."

"If that's what you want," he replied, sliding the swim trunks down his body and hopping into the steady stream of the shower.

She watched as he yanked the shower curtain closed, obviously still upset with her. She hated that she'd ruined his plans, but the hotel and the small town it was in would be much better for the two of them. She might even do some research after dinner to find a resort somewhere close. She'd pay for the change in destination if necessary. It was the least she could do for her boyfriend who'd tried to do so much already.

She drove the rental to the store she recognized from their first destination after the airport. Brad had taken her inside. They'd practically bought the whole store. She'd watched in horror as he'd shown her the backpack, sleeping bags, and cooking items they'd need, along with those terrible iodine tablets and metal canteens. They'd used some of it. Those items they couldn't return. She'd left them in the trunk. She carried in several bags of the things they hadn't used and headed toward the counter.

"Oh, you don't want that," a woman said from off to the side of the counter.

"I'm sorry?" Adler asked, turning toward the voice.

The woman was striking, with light blonde hair and bright blue eyes. She looked to be around Adler's age; maybe a year or two older or younger. She was athletic in build, but not overly so. She wore a tight-fitting white V-neck shirt with a small pocket over her left breast and a pair of jeans with well-worn sneakers. Adler realized she'd looked the woman up and down. She met the woman's eyes hoping she hadn't noticed.

"That jerky brand is terrible," the woman said, pointing to the three packs of beef jerky Brad had bought for the expedition. "There's one that I recommend on my tours. If you like the spicy kind, theirs is pretty hot."

"Hot?" Adler questioned, gulping for some reason.

"The jerky," the woman said with a smile. "It's spicy."

"Oh, right," Adler replied, looking down at the half-open bag and its contents. "I'm actually just returning it."

"Because it's terrible?" the woman asked, taking a few steps toward her.

"No, I haven't tried it."

"Then, why are you returning it?"

"Because we–"

"Can I help you?" a young man approached from what must have been a back office, and asked.

"I need to return these things. I have the receipt."

"Okay," he replied, taking the paper from her.

"I'll leave you alone," the woman said.

"No, you don't–" Adler turned to face her. "Trip got canceled. That's why I'm returning."

"Oh, that sucks," the woman said. "You came all the way here and you have to leave?"

"Not leaving. I'm just not camping, so I don't need these things anymore. I'm staying in Jackson Hole." She left out the fact that she'd considered leaving only twenty minutes ago while arguing with her boyfriend in their hotel room. "At least for now."

"It's a great town."

"You're from here?"

"No, I'm from South Lake Tahoe. I'm here on business."

"Here you go," the man behind the counter handed her the receipt with another one stapled to it. "The refund will go back on the original card within five to seven business days."

"Thank you," Adler replied, turning back to the woman. "What business are you in?"

The woman looked toward the man, nodded to the side, and started walking toward the door. Adler followed her without thought, tucking the receipt into her jeans pocket. They made their way to the front of the store, where the woman pretended to look at socks.

"I'm in this business," she said softly. "Outdoor equipment. I'm here checking out the competition."

"Really? How industrious of you," Adler said with a smile.

"I'm thinking of opening a store here. It's a competitive market. I'm here taking a look at all the shops and trying to decide on a location."

"You own a store?"

"It's a family business, but I've officially taken it over. We have three locations now, but all of them are around the lake. I'm hoping to expand a little further."

"Well, I hope it works out," Adler said.

The blue eyes met her own gray ones. The woman had this soft but, still, seemingly strong expression on her face that communicated something to Adler without her having said anything.

"I'm Morgan, by the way."

"Adler," she replied, holding out her hand for Morgan to shake.

"Are you here by yourself?" Morgan asked.

"No, with my boyfriend. He's back at the hotel," she said.

"Jerky?"

"It was his, yes." Adler laughed and ran her hand through her light brown hair, wishing she'd showered before coming out after all. "I disappointed him because I am not a big camper."

"No?"

"Not even a little bit." Adler smiled as she looked out the window. "I thought we were going on a romantic get-away. He took me on a seven-mile hike into the middle of nowhere and made me pee behind a tree."

Morgan laughed and said, "Camping *can* be romantic if you do it right."

"Yeah?"

"I used to go with my girlfriend all the time. Well, she's my ex-girlfriend now and engaged to another woman. They go on romantic camping trips now."

Adler caught the word *girlfriend*. It didn't bother her at all. Her sister Paxton was gay. Adler remembered Paxton coming out to her. She'd worried her big sister and their parents wouldn't accept her, which was ridiculous because she was family. It didn't matter who she found happiness with as long as she found happiness.

"What makes them romantic?" Adler asked, changing the subject slightly.

"The person, I guess. That's the first step." Morgan's eyes got big. "Not that I'm suggesting your boyfriend isn't the right person."

"It's okay," Adler replied. "Go on."

"Well, I think it's all about the preparation. You plan it together. You bring all the things that would make a night of romance for you as a couple."

"For instance?" Adler asked, suddenly interested.

"Like, your music." The woman removed a pair of socks from a hook and moved them to a different hook. "Those go here."

"This is your competition. Should you be helping them?"

"I'm not an asshole," Morgan said. "And you should have that special song you share on standby along with some of the classics. You make sure you bring those flameless candles and get a tent a little bigger than you really need to make room for them. A lantern is nice, but candles everywhere really set the mood."

"You sound like a pro at this," Adler replied with a chuckle.

Morgan looked at her and replied, "I love the outdoors. I've not had many opportunities to get out in it recently. Business has been booming, which is a great problem to have. I'm just not the one leading the tours anymore. I have tour guides that do that while I come here to explore the competition."

"You're right next to a national park. You're not going to explore?"

"I might. I've just had a lot of work to do, with the new outposts we have around the lake for kayak and canoe rentals. We've got eight of them now, and they don't have managers. It's basically a few teenage boys running them."

"Keeps you busy, though. I know I love my work for that reason."

"What do you do?"

"I'm a COO at a food distributor," she answered.

"COO? Nice," Morgan said, clearly impressed.

"Says the CEO," Adler replied with a smile.

"I'm not a CEO."

"You're running an empire there, Morgan. What else should I call you?"

"Just Morgan," the woman replied.

"Well, *just Morgan*, you are very impressive," Adler said.

"As are you," Morgan replied. "Listen, what are you doing right now? Do you want to grab something to eat?"

"I can't," Adler began. "Sorry. Brad's waiting for me back at the hotel."

"No apology necessary; I understand," she said. "But if you're hanging around town and in any interest of killing time with coffee or something, maybe we could hang out. I'm here alone for the week."

"That sounds good. Let me give you my number. I'm assuming cell phones work in this tiny town?"

"They do," Morgan replied through a laugh. "They even have the internet here. Did you know that?"

Adler laughed as Morgan pulled out her phone to enter her contact information.

CHAPTER 2

MORGAN made her notes on her phone as she sat waiting in the café. She'd been in Jackson Hole, Wyoming, for over a week, and had at least one more week to go before she'd pack and go back to South Lake. The last store she'd visited had been pretty extensively stocked. They even offered the usual tours and some more interesting historical ones for the town. They stocked the main three brands for the majority of the items. She was glad they didn't stock the one brand she'd loved the most and had stocked in her own store, since she'd taken it over from her parents. It would give her the edge if she did decide to open a store here.

She finished typing and looked at her to-do list. She had a meeting later that afternoon with the real estate agent, who'd been showing her around the listings she was interested in. There were four available spaces that could work. A fifth space was a little too small, but they'd still gone to see it anyway. There were also three lots available just outside of town, but they were on the way to the park. She could build from scratch, but that would delay the opening by longer than she'd wanted. They'd still go see them. She wanted to make the best decision for the business which had been dominating her life for the past several years. To do that, she needed to know all her options.

"Hey," Adler said.

"Oh, hey," Morgan replied, looking up at her with a smile.

"Can I sit?"

"Go for it," Morgan said, motioning to the chair in front of her small table. "I would have ordered for you, but I didn't know what you like."

"Skim lattes are my drink. Can I get you a refill?"

"Same is fine," Morgan replied.

She watched as Adler walked to the counter and ordered from a college-aged barista, who definitely was taken aback by how attractive the woman in front of him was. Adler's eyes were a gray that could only be described as rare. Maybe it wasn't all that rare, but Morgan hadn't seen it before. They weren't just gray. They were a pool of lights and darks that swam together to mesmerize anyone who caught their gaze. Morgan sat her phone on the table and turned to stare out the window instead. Adler was a beautiful woman, but she was also a beautiful straight woman on vacation with her boyfriend.

"Here you go," Adler said as she placed a paper coffee cup in front of Morgan.

"Thanks. I'll get your next one," she replied.

"I'm glad you called. I needed to get out of the hotel." Adler took a sip of her coffee.

"Everything okay?" Morgan asked.

"Brad and I aren't exactly having the best anniversary trip."

"Anniversary?"

"This was his gift to me for our one year. I was already on thin ice because I kept pushing it off. It's been six months, and he finally got me to take time away from work. It hasn't gone how he'd planned."

"Well, you did return the man's beef jerky. What did you expect?"

Adler laughed with hot coffee in her mouth causing her to cough her laughter and place the cup back on the table.

"I didn't know he liked beef jerky until he bought the stuff the other day."

"But he likes the outdoors enough to bring you here for a vacation?"

"He's been camping before, I guess. I didn't know that until we had hours of hiking to get through and nothing else to talk about. He's a great guy. He puts up with me, and I am *not* easy to put up with."

"Why?" Morgan sipped on her coffee.

"I'm a workaholic. I'm one of those strange people that actually like their job. I love being a COO. I knew I wanted to be in business operations all through my undergrad. I didn't care what type of company; I just knew I wanted to run the show. The next step is CEO, and I'm one retirement away from being the youngest in the history of my company. It means I work long hours. And even when I'm home, I'm still sometimes working. That's not something everyone can handle."

"I know all about that. One of the reasons my ex and I broke up was because I was working so much toward the end. I had just taken a more active role in the business. And I had less and less time for her, which meant I had less time to plan romantic camping trips or even remember that it was an anniversary. I love my stores, though. Reese understands that. We're still friends, which is amazing. I just wasn't interested in sacrificing what I saw for the future of the business for a relationship. I know that sounds terrible."

"Not to me. It's my every day. I've lost three other serious boyfriends because of work. One of them worked with me. When I got promoted above him, he couldn't handle it. The other two just wanted a girlfriend who could be home for dinner. I'm not that girlfriend."

"What do you think will happen when you meet that person that you want to spend every moment with? Do you think you'd be willing to give something up at work if work is a problem?" Morgan asked.

"I see you're assuming Brad is not that someone, since he and I have already met," Adler replied.

"Shit... I'm sorry. I keep doing that," Morgan said. "Sorry."

"It's okay," Adler returned with a smile. "I think he just really loves me."

"That's a good thing, right?"

"Yes, of course. It just means he struggles when I'm not around or when I'm really busy, which is a lot of the time. I promised him I'd leave work behind and go on this vacation with him." She paused on a sigh. "I've been the worst girlfriend. I've complained non-stop and got caught checking my email yesterday."

"Couldn't leave it behind after all?"

"I really was just checking what had come in since we'd arrived, and replying to a few of the important ones. But I'm sure it doesn't seem that way to him. Dinner wasn't fun last night. We ordered room service. He ate on the balcony. I ate on the sofa in the room. It's not exactly the romantic getaway he was hoping for so far."

"What's he doing right now?"

"He went for a run. We woke up and went downstairs for the hotel breakfast. He said he wanted to watch some game. I let him do that while I watched a sappy romantic chick flick on my laptop with my headphones in. Then, he went for a run. You called. I came here."

"You should do something nice for him," Morgan suggested. "To make it up to him."

"I should. You're right. What do I do?"

"What does he like?" Morgan asked.

"He's a contractor with his own company. He likes, I don't know, man things." She shrugged.

Morgan laughed and replied, "Man things?"

"Yes, man things."

"How am I supposed to respond to that?" Morgan asked.

"Give me an idea of what to do to make it up to him."

Morgan took a drink of her coffee as she considered and said, "Take him to a movie."

"A movie?"

"There's a theater down the street. I saw they were playing a new Tom Cruise movie. There's bound to be some manly action scenes and partial female nudity."

Adler laughed again. Morgan looked away from the woman again. Leave it to Morgan to find a straight woman she could never have so attractive, her mouth had gone dry, despite having had two cups of coffee.

"That's not a bad idea."

"And tomorrow, go on one of the hiking tours or something. Think of it as a compromise: you're not peeing behind a tree, but you're not just stuck in a hotel, either."

"Am I crazy? Shouldn't he want to be stuck in a hotel with me for two weeks?" Adler asked. "It's an anniversary trip. Shouldn't we be tearing off each other's clothes every chance we get?"

"If he's not interested in tearing off your clothes, there's something wrong with him." Morgan's eyes got big like they had the day before, when they'd been talking in the store. "That came out wrong."

"It's okay," Adler replied. "And thank you."

"I'm sure you guys will be fine. Just maybe knock off the work stuff unless you know for sure you won't get caught," Morgan suggested.

"What do you have going on for the rest of the day?" Adler asked.

"I'm going with a realtor to check out a few listings for the future store."

"That sounds like fun," Adler said and appeared to mean it.

"It is. If you're not busy, you can tag along. I'm sure you and Brad have plans, though."

"We don't, actually. I mean, I might try to do the action movie with partial nudity thing and dinner before or after, but he hasn't called to let me know he's back. I'm free until then."

"And you really want to spend your time looking at empty buildings with me?" Morgan asked.

"Can I put on my COO hat and ask the realtor a lot of questions?" Adler asked with a smile.

"Definitely. I don't have a COO; I could use the assist," Morgan said.

"Done."

CHAPTER 3

"WHERE have you been?" Brad asked when she returned to the hotel several hours later.

"I went to coffee with Morgan. I left you a note."

"Who's Morgan?" he asked, shifting from his position on the small, beige sofa.

"A woman I met when I was returning the stuff yesterday. I told you about her last night," she answered, feeling a little attacked.

"Adler, what's going on with us?" He turned off the TV and gave her his full attention.

"Nothing."

"Really? I had to beg you to come here, and that was before you even knew it was a camping trip. You only agreed because I pressured you to do it before my project starts up."

"That's not true, Brad." She sat next to him on the sofa. "I wanted a vacation. This wasn't what I was expecting. I'm doing the best that I can here."

"The best you can? This is supposed to be something romantic that the two of us do, and you're doing the best you can?"

"Brad, come on." She placed her hand hesitantly on his thigh. "You know this isn't me. This vacation is a vacation that you would like, and that's fine. It's just not what I wanted in my first real vacation in years. Am I wrong for expecting we'd relax somewhere with an ocean view?"

"No, you're not wrong. I guess I was just trying something new. I was hoping I could get you to like this stuff."

"What stuff? Since when are you even into this stuff?" she asked, removing her hand.

"I'm almost forty, Adler," he said it as if it should mean something. Then, it did. "I like my life, but it's also kind of boring."

"Boring?" she asked, leaning away from him.

"I've got a great job and a great girlfriend. Don't get me wrong: I love what I have. But it's the same every day. I wanted something different for once. I wanted to get outside and really enjoy it."

"And you thought our anniversary trip was the best time for that? Why didn't you just plan a guy's trip or something?"

"I don't know. I was stupid," he replied with a short laugh. "I was thinking we could go out for a nice dinner in town. I made a reservation. When we got back, we could look at flights to just go home."

"Home?"

"It's pretty obvious you don't want to be here. We can just go home. I don't know. Maybe we can stay in a fancy hotel in the city for a few nights for our anniversary."

Adler looked down at her hands, which were tightly clasped in her lap. She'd spent the entire afternoon with Morgan Burns. They'd shared another cup of coffee, talked about their lives, and then gone to meet Morgan's realtor. They'd visited two locations. One was an existing structure. The other was an empty lot. Morgan asked all the right questions. Adler had tossed in a few of her own for good measure. They'd laughed and talked more on the drive back to the café where Morgan had dropped her off at the rental car. They'd agreed to meet up the following afternoon if Brad and she didn't have any finite plans. As she thought about that potential meeting, she knew she didn't want to leave Jackson Hole just yet.

"How about I take *you* out tonight?" she asked. "We can do dinner and a movie. There's an action movie playing at the theater. We haven't done that in forever."

"Action movie?" He smirked at her.

"With possible partial female nudity, I've been told," she added.

"You had me at action," he said.

"Let's maybe go for a short hike tomorrow morning. After breakfast, we can head out and do a mile or two or something."

"Really?"

"Sure. I told Morgan I'd meet her in the afternoon. Is that okay?"

"You really like this woman, huh?" he asked, leaning toward her to kiss her on the cheek. "And I'll get dressed for dinner. I didn't exactly bring a suit and tie. I hope they'll take me in jeans and a T-shirt."

"I do like her," Adler said as he marched toward the suitcase on the luggage rack.

"What?" he asked, not looking up at her. "Oh, right. Morgan. Is she from here?"

"No, she's from Lake Tahoe," she replied, standing and removing something from her pocket at the same time. "She's here for work for the next few days. I know it's our trip, but I was kind of hoping I could spend some time with her before she goes if that's okay with you. I think she might be a good friend one day."

"Yeah?" He looked up at her as he pulled off his shirt. "Maybe."

"Well, that's good. You hardly have time for me, let alone friends. I think it's a good thing."

As he headed into the bathroom, likely to put on more deodorant and fix his hair for dinner, she tucked something into the pocket of her carry-on bag. For some reason, such a small, inexpensive item had meaning to her. She planned on keeping it. Brad didn't need to know about it. He wouldn't understand why she'd want to hang on to it anyway.

***

"How'd action movie and dinner go last night?" Morgan asked Adler the following afternoon as they rounded a corner after eating a late lunch together at one of the local pizza places.

"He fell asleep," she replied.

"What?" Morgan laughed. "When? During the movie?"

"No, right after. We went to dinner first. The movie was fine, but not my thing. It was for him, anyway. We got back to the hotel then."

"Where, I'm assuming, you were hoping for a little more than sleep?" Morgan guessed.

Adler laughed back and replied, "He said he was exhausted and passed out on the bed without even taking his shoes and socks off."

"Let me guess... You took them off for him?"

"How'd you know?"

"You just seem like the kind of woman who wouldn't like things on the bed," Morgan said.

"I do?"

"Oh, yeah." Morgan laughed again. "We're here." She pointed at a building with a *'for sale'* sign in the expansive storefront window. "And is that a guy thing? Socks in bed? I understand when it's freezing and you're wearing them to keep warm, but I've heard from my straight friend, Stacy, that her husband has sex with nothing on but his socks."

"So, you wouldn't know, I take it? Men in bed, I mean?" Adler asked, feeling her cheeks redden.

"No, I wouldn't." Morgan pulled open the door for her and followed behind. "Only women for me. Socks for warmth, I understand. Sex is an activity, though, that doesn't generally get people cold enough to require footwear."

Adler laughed and replied, "So, women don't wear socks during sex?"

"Do you?" Morgan asked her.

"I guess not," Adler said. "Where's the realtor?"

"She said she'd meet me here. What do you think?" Morgan looked around the completely empty space. "Imagine it with stuff in it, obviously."

"So, you don't sell invisible sporting goods?" Adler asked with a smile.

"Yes, you just knocked over an entire aisle of ski poles." Morgan pointed at nothing behind Adler. "So, what's on the agenda tonight?"

"What do you mean?" Adler asked.

"With you and Brad. You guys went on a short hike this morning. He let me borrow you for lunch and this. What are you guys up to tonight?"

"I don't know. We haven't made any official plans."

"You should go dancing or something. Does he dance?"

"I don't dance."

"You don't dance?" Morgan asked.

"Not since high school, no."

"Homecoming queen?" Morgan pointed at her with a lifted eyebrow.

"No."

"Prom?"

"No, homecoming court, but not queen. I wasn't on the prom court."

"Cheerleader?" Morgan asked.

"No. You?"

"God, no. Softball." She shrugged. "I fit the stereotype in many ways."

"Soccer," Adler said.

"You played soccer?"

"My sister and I both did. She was a striker. I was a goalie. Things were always interesting when we played in the backyard growing up. She was a way better swimmer, though. Me, not so much," Adler said.

"Yeah?" Morgan looked away as the door opened behind them. "Hey, Sandy."

"Hi there. Are you ready to have a look around?" Sandy, the realtor, asked.

"I noticed we're a little off the main drag," Adler said. "What kind of foot traffic would a store get here? We only walked over because we knew where we were going. But I didn't see anyone else around."

Morgan looked at her in surprise and said, "Great question."

***

"Brad decided to hang out with some guys he met tonight," Adler said.

"Yeah?"

"I guess he went to a bar and played darts with them. That's what the text says, anyway." She held up her phone to her new friend. "My night appears to be open."

"What do you want to do?" Morgan asked.

"I could work at the hotel since he'll be out for a few hours."

"Wrong," Morgan replied, sliding her arm through Adler's as they walked side by side. "I have a better idea. You interested?"

"I'm not good with surprises."

"I didn't say it was a surprise. I'll tell you what it is once you agree to go."

"That doesn't seem fair," Adler replied with a chuckle. "It sounds eerily similar to a surprise."

"Not a surprise, but you will need to change first," Morgan said.

CHAPTER 4

SHE really needed to stop this. Adler Williams was a beautiful woman that Morgan had now spent way too much time with. Adler was supposed to be on a romantic trip with her boyfriend. Her boyfriend was a man. Adler liked men. Well, she liked one man. She loved him. They'd been together for over a year. That was the stage where most people were living together or even engaged. Morgan needed to stop, but she only had one more night in Jackson Hole. She'd be boarding her short flight back to South Lake tomorrow in the afternoon. If she only had one more night in town, though, she knew how she wanted to spend it. It wasn't alone in her hotel room.

"I warned you, right?" Adler asked. "I'm not really the outdoorsy type, Morgan."

"I know. But I told you, there's a way to do it right," Morgan said.

"Where are we going now that you've gotten me all dressed up for a night in a tent?"

"I've got my gear in the rental SUV. We're going to a place I've been to a few times when I came to Grand Teton for fun; not work. It's mostly a drive up until there's a short hike from the campsite."

"Campsite? Morgan, I only have a few hours before Brad gets back. It's already six. He'd probably hang out with whomever he met until about ten or eleven at the latest. I might even need to have the rental ready to drive him back to the hotel if he's drinking."

"That's what cabs and shared rides are for," Morgan

said. "He'll be fine." She turned to face Adler as the car stopped at a traffic light. "The drive up is only about thirty minutes. Then, we'll park, and you can use the bathrooms at the site if that makes you feel better than going behind a tree. "The sun sets so late here this time of year; we'll have a great view. It's only about a mile away from the main site, I promise."

"Okay. I trust you," Adler replied.

Morgan turned away, back toward the street, upon hearing those words. She drove them through the green light and turned toward the national park she'd visited several times in her youth and a few more since graduating college. She'd come to this particular national park after Reese had broken up with her. She'd made the nearly twelve-hour drive, spent three days camping and hiking by herself, and drove back. Nature hadn't healed her how she'd hoped, but it was a start.

They climbed the road through the thick trees, following behind a truck with a trailer hitched to it. It took them closer to forty-five minutes, but it had been worth it. Morgan had looked over at Adler several times during their silent interludes. Every so often, one of them would say something. Sometimes, it was about something out the window. Other times, it was small talk in an attempt to get to know one another more. Morgan parked the car in one of the few empty spots. They both got out of the car and walked around to the back where Morgan had stowed the gear.

"I brought everything just in case. Well, I always bring everything," Morgan said, shouldering a pack.

"This is enough stuff for a week," Adler remarked, shouldering a smaller pack that Morgan passed her.

"No, it's enough stuff for about two nights. Sometimes, when I travel, I just camp instead of staying in a hotel. I brought this stuff to do that, and I haven't yet."

"Will you, tonight?"

"I guess that's up to you," Morgan replied, taking the

tent she'd rented and looping it over her other shoulder. "It's my last night here."

"I thought you were staying for another week," Adler replied, seemingly concerned.

Morgan smiled and replied, "I said that about four days ago, Adler. I fly back tomorrow afternoon. If I'm going to camp here, I need to do it tonight."

"Morgan, you shouldn't be wasting your last night on me," Adler said, following Morgan out of the small lot.

"I'd hardly call this a waste, Addie," Morgan replied. "Oh, sorry. I guess I just decided on a nickname for you. Is that okay?" She turned back to Adler.

"It's fine. But, Morgan, let's just check out this view you wanted to show me. You can drive me back down and come back up."

"I can't," Morgan replied. "There are rules about coming up after the sun sets. We can go down, but if I drove you back into town, I wouldn't be able to come back to the park tonight. Come on. It's this way." She pointed through an open field with a smattering of different-sized tents. "It's through those trees."

Adler didn't say anything else. She followed Morgan past people who were playing card games with their children at picnic tables, and others, who were setting up their equipment or fires for the night. When they arrived at the start of the trail, Morgan motioned to Adler to go first.

"Me?"

"Yes, you," Morgan answered with a laugh. "It's a pretty straight trail. It ends at the water. You can't mess it up."

"If you say so," Adler replied.

She walked ahead of Morgan through the trees that were still full of summer leaves. Every now and then, Morgan heard one of the smaller animals scamper off with their arriving footsteps. The sun shone brightly in the sky but was on its way to the horizon with every step they took. She so badly wanted Adler to see this. This view was *the* view. Whenever Morgan needed a moment of solace, she'd think of this view. When they emerged from the trees minutes later, she moved to stand beside Adler. She wanted to see her take this place in. It was important to Morgan, for reasons she couldn't quite understand, that Adler find this place just as special as she did.

**

"Oh, my God," Adler whispered as her wide eyes moved from left to right to take in the scene.

In front of them was a small field with a few down trees here and there. It wasn't a beach, exactly. There was no white sand, but the water in front of them was clear. The dark green grass at their feet gave way to a thinner layer of light green blades before it changed to small pebbles. Then, the water took over. Beyond the water, far off into the distance, Adler took in the Tetons. They reflected perfectly into the clear water, making it appear as if there were two sets of three facing one another as if in a duel for mountain superiority. Just before the mountains was a beach –if she could call it that – not unlike the one they were currently standing on, and rows and rows of bright green trees. The middle mountain was the largest. It was gray, with a few places covered in white snow. The two smaller mountains stood so strong on either side, offering the same beauty.

"It's not bad, huh?" Morgan asked in the silence between them.

"Not bad? Morgan, it's gorgeous."

"It's my favorite place maybe in the world," Morgan said.

Adler turned to Morgan then. She'd spent the entirety of their time here staring off in the distance. She'd failed to take in Morgan's reaction. She wanted to see Morgan's reaction to her most favorite place. Morgan's blue eyes were brighter, if that was even possible. Her smile was close-lipped but met her eyes. Adler watched her inhale deeply, taking in the pure air of the mountains. Adler was certain that this was one of those moments she'd remember forever; not merely because of the scenery, but because of Morgan taking it in with her.

"It's perfect," Adler said a moment later before turning her eyes away from Morgan.

"We can eat here if you want," Morgan offered. "It's not five-star cuisine, but I packed what I like to prepare out here."

"Please don't tell me you have ramen," Adler replied.

"Ramen? I haven't eaten that stuff since college."

Adler laughed and said, "It's what Brad and I had the other night."

"Well, I figured I'd be out here tonight. I brought all the stuff I need to make a kickass meal. You're not a vegetarian, are you?"

"No," Adler said.

"Then, you can help get the fire ready. You can do that, right?"

"I can build a fire, yes. I *was* a Girl Scout," Adler told her.

"*You* were a Girl Scout?" Morgan asked, dropping the bags she'd brought and tossing the tent bag off to the side.

"I was, yes."

"But you hate camping," Morgan said.

"I don't hate camping. I just haven't been since I was a little kid. I spend my days in the city, that's true. I haven't had to build a fire since I was fourteen and went to Girl Scout camp. I earned a badge, though."

"For fire building?"

"Yes, for fire building. I had a lot of badges."

"Of course, you did," Morgan said, laughing. "Can you get it going? There's a starter in the pack you carried."

"A starter? Am I a rookie?" Adler tossed back.

Morgan laughed as Adler walked around the field collecting small sticks, returning them to a pile. Then, she ventured out a little further into the tree line to retrieve a few bigger sticks and a couple of logs. Adler built the strong base

of the fire, layering it with the smaller sticks in the pit someone else had left behind. She tried and tried to use the old-
fashioned approach she'd learned at camp to get the fire
started. Morgan worked to prepare their dinner. They worked
in silence for several more minutes before Adler sat back on
her heels, giving up.

"Hey, rookie." Morgan sat next to her. "How about
that starter?" Morgan asked.

She didn't laugh, though. She just reached beyond
Adler and pulled out a small brick and a long lighter. She
handed both to Adler and left her alone to start the fire.
Adler lit the starter, placing it into the center of the pit. She
coaxed the flames by blowing on them until she had a de-
cent-sized fire. Morgan came over then and set out the
cooking materials. It was then that Adler noticed there were
chicken and some kind of slaw in plastic bags. Morgan set a
grate over the fire. Adler watched her place several pieces of
chicken on top of it once it had reached the appropriate
temperature.

"You prepared this in advance?" Adler asked.

"It's easier that way. When I just do a night or two, I
can freeze things and have a cooler with me. I usually get at
least one or two really good meals this way."

"It looks great. Smells good, too."

"It's a whiskey barbeque sauce. The slaw is ready. I just
need to put the dressing in that bag. If you do that in advance, it goes bad faster. Can you toss it all together for me?"

"Sure," Adler replied.

Adler took one plastic bag, opened it, and added the
dressing for the slaw. She tossed the ingredients together.
Morgan turned the chicken and brushed it with what looked
like barbeque sauce. When Adler returned, she watched Morgan plate the slaw on metal plates. The woman produced
silverware next, passing them to Adler. Once the chicken
was done, she added a breast and a thigh to Adler's plate
before doing the same to her own.

"Do you want to eat by the water?" Morgan asked.

"I'm actually okay where we are," Adler replied, meaning every word.

They were seated on a large log someone had moved to act as a bench for the fire pit. The log faced the pristine view as the sun continued its quest for the horizon.

"What do you think?" Morgan asked after several minutes.

"What's in this sauce? It's amazing," Adler replied.

"Whiskey," Morgan said.

"Whiskey?"

"The alcohol cooks off. Don't worry. I'm not trying to get either of us drunk. I did, however, bring several bottles of water. Want one?"

"Please," Adler replied. "But let me get them."

Adler returned moments later with a bottle for each of them. They ate in relative silence. Adler couldn't take her eyes off the view.

"You okay?" Morgan asked when she'd finished eating.

"Why?"

"Because you've been staring at me for, like, five minutes." She laughed and sat her plate on the ground in front of her. "If we're planning on leaving tonight, we have about thirty more minutes. Once the sun is completely gone, it's not as easy to get back, but it's doable. We just don't want to be hiking long after that."

"If?" Adler asked.

"We can stay, Addie." Morgan turned to face the water.

CHAPTER 5

"STAY the night?" Adler asked.

"We have all we need. I was planning on staying out here, anyway." Morgan shrugged. "It's beautiful in the morning. We could watch the sun come up."

Morgan knew she was asking a lot. Adler only agreed to come out here for a few hours. Morgan was asking her to sleep outside. She was asking her to spend the night away from her boyfriend. She knew Adler would say no, but something inside her was burning to ask.

"Okay," Adler replied.

"Okay?" Morgan asked, surprised.

"I just need to let Brad know. I don't want him to worry."

"You should be able to get reception here. We're not that high up," Morgan replied. "Do you want to call him?"

"I should," Adler said. "Can you give me a minute?"

"I can do better than that. I left some stuff in the truck you might need. I have an extra toothbrush and things like that. How about I go back and get it? We can meet at the bathrooms in, like, twenty minutes. We can take care of as much as we can there; then, walk back and get the tent set up. It's pretty easy. You will, likely, still have to pee behind a tree later, though," Morgan said.

"I'll call Brad and meet you there," Adler replied with a small laugh.

Morgan nodded and took off for the trail. She turned back to see Adler putting the phone to her ear. She turned back to the woods quickly. She didn't want to hear Adler talking to her boyfriend. She knew they'd likely exchange words to one another that would only hurt Morgan. She smacked her forehead at the thought. She should turn back and tell Adler she'd changed her mind. She should turn back to tell her she'd rather camp alone or that she'd just stay in a hotel tonight. Morgan couldn't, though. She kept walking instead.

***

"Hey, it's me. Listen, I'm still with Morgan. I'm sure you just didn't hear the phone ring because you're in a loud bar. I'm thinking about staying at Morgan's place tonight. We're–" She stared at the water, trying to consider how to lie only a little bit instead of a lot. "We're watching movies and eating popcorn in her vacation rental. I've had a little wine, and I think it's safer for me to sleep on her sofa. If you drink too much, call a car. I'll text you tomorrow when I'm leaving." That was *not* a small lie. "I–" She looked at the ground. "I'll see you tomorrow. Good night."

She hung up, stared at the ground, and kicked a rock. She looked back up at the sky, which was a mixture of lively colors. She could just make the moon out, as if it was behind the curtain of a stage, waiting to come out on a cue. She waited another few moments, watching the fire they'd built dwindle somewhat. She added another log and a few twigs, wondering if they were allowed to leave it burning without them being here. Then, she wondered about leaving their stuff unattended. There was no one around. She was completely alone. She inhaled deeply, smelling the pine and the fire. She turned to the woods and took the path back to Morgan.

"All good?" Morgan asked when she met her at the bathrooms.

"I left a message. He didn't answer."

"Is that okay? I can still take you back," Morgan replied, handing her a small bag.

"I'm sure he's just having a good time," Adler said. "I just left your stuff out there. Is that okay?"

"We'll only be a minute. That's the only trail that goes

that way. So, unless someone just happens upon it going through the woods, we're fine."

Adler used the borrowed supplies while Morgan used what she'd packed. They headed back down the trail together, past the families and couples that were sitting by their fires talking and laughing. Adler watched a man of about twenty-five sling his arm over the shoulder of his female companion. She thought about Brad, wondering if that had been his plan the other night. Then, she thought about the lie she'd told him in her message. Had she told him she was spending the night out here with Morgan, when she'd given him such a terrible time about his plan, it would have broken his heart. It would be even worse because she had no explanation for why she wanted to be out here with Morgan and not her boyfriend.

She helped Morgan pitch the tent, which took only a few minutes. They added more fuel to the fire. Morgan packed up everything that might attract bears or other animals and walked to the locked container yards away from their site. When she returned, Adler already had most of their stuff inside the tent. She rolled out the one sleeping bag Morgan had brought, not anticipating a companion for the night. Morgan also had two fleece blankets and a sleeping pad that would separate them from the ground below and keep the coolness away from them during the night.

The lantern was needed once the sun was almost gone. Morgan turned it on slightly, leaving it in the tent. Then, she ushered Adler outside. They stood next to one another as the sun finished its journey. Adler wondered when she'd ever felt so at peace in her life. She couldn't think of a single moment that felt as good as this one. Morgan's hand moved to the small of her back. Adler stood frozen in time.

"We should get in the tent soon. The bugs will be out in full force. Plus, it's going to get cold." Her hand moved away.

"Right," Adler replied, missing the contact.

They moved back inside the tent. Morgan zipped it up

but left the outer screen part open, in order to enjoy the view just a few more minutes before the darkness enveloped them completely.

"I brought cards. Want to play?" Morgan asked.

"Cards?"

"Poker?"

"With just two people?" Adler asked with a smile.

"We could play war instead. I should warn you though: I'm very good," Morgan said with a smirk.

"At a game of chance?"

"War isn't a game of chance," Morgan countered.

"It's literally flipping cards over and hoping that your card is higher."

"And you think that's chance?"

"Unless you're cheating. Do you cheat?" Adler asked. Then, she understood the weight of the question she'd just asked. "I mean–"

"I don't." Morgan pulled out the deck of cards from a side pocket of her pack. "You want to cut the deck?"

They played war for several hands until Morgan claimed a three out of five victory. By then, darkness was all around them. Sounds of howling came from the trees behind them. Adler was also getting cold. She hadn't thought this through. She was wearing wool socks and her hiking boots since that was what she'd worn that day. She had on one of the two hooded sweatshirts she owned, with a T-shirt under it, along with a pair of old jeans. She pulled the hood up over her ears, causing Morgan to smile at her.

"What? I'm cold."

"I can see that. Hold on." Morgan reached into her backpack and removed a long-sleeved shirt. She pulled out a pair of long underwear as well, passing them to Adler. "Put these on. It's better to sleep naked, though."

"What?" Adler asked, taking the clothes.

"Body heat. The sleeping bag is designed to keep you warm. It's better to sleep in your underwear and nothing else."

"So, you'll be–"

"Sleeping in my underwear, yes." Morgan looked down for a minute. "You can take the sleeping bag if you want. I can take the blankets. I'll be fine wearing what I'm wearing. That's an extra set of long underwear. Would that make you more comfortable?"

"What if we put the blankets under us and the sleeping bag on top?"

"We can do that, but you'll still want to put those on." She nodded toward the long underwear. "I'll turn away."

Adler watched as Morgan turned to face the tent. Her hair was pulled back into a ponytail, but after she turned, she undid it. Her blonde hair fell over her back. Adler turned her head to the left before she swallowed hard. She pulled off her sweatshirt quickly, sliding the long-sleeved shirt on over her T-shirt. She balled her sweatshirt up and placed it where her head would fall. She unbuttoned and unzipped her jeans, lay down, and slid them off her legs. She'd forgotten she still had her boots on, though. Before she could sit back up, Morgan had turned her head slightly at her struggle.

"I got it."

Morgan untied Adler's shoes and pulled each of them off. She turned her head to Adler, smiling as she did. Her eyes lowered for a millisecond before she turned away, back to the side of the tent. Adler slid the pants over her legs, tossing her jeans to the side. She sat back up.

"I'm dressed," she said then.

Morgan turned and replied, "Ready for sleep?"

"It's, like, eight or something." Adler lay down, following Morgan's lead.

"We can talk for a while until you fall asleep," Morgan said. She turned on her side, reached for the sleeping bag she'd unzipped all the way, and pulled it over them just as Adler turned to face her. "What do you want to talk about?"

"What time are you leaving tomorrow?"

"My flight is at five-fifteen," Morgan said softly. "I should be at the airport by four."

"Do you need a ride?" Adler asked.

"I have to return the rental."

"Oh, right," she said.

"Besides, you have a boyfriend waiting for you at a hotel," Morgan returned and looked away from her.

"He's still out with his new friends." Adler slid a little closer. "And I'm with mine."

"I'm your new friend?" Morgan asked.

"I hope so," Adler replied. "I know you're leaving tomorrow, but you have my number. We can still talk, right?"

"Sure," Morgan said. "And if you're ever in Tahoe, you have a place to stay."

"Do you ever get to Seattle?" Adler asked.

"I've never been, no."

"You should come. You'd have a place to stay there, obviously."

"You've got some fancy place there, don't you? Let me guess... It's a two-bedroom penthouse. You seem like a modern kind of woman. Brad, I'm guessing here, is more traditional. Does he have like a deer head above the fireplace or something?"

"Brad has his own place," Adler replied. "And I don't live in the penthouse. I'm on the twelfth floor."

"And how many floors are there?" Morgan asked.

"Thirteen."

"Oh, I apologize." Morgan laughed.

"You should." Adler laughed, too.

"Why don't you and Brad live together?"

"Is there some rule that says you have to move in with someone after a certain period of time?" She rolled onto her back.

"No," Morgan replied, raising her head up on her elbow to look down at the woman beside her.

Adler looked up at her, taking in the flickering lantern light in her blue eyes.

"I've just gotten used to living alone, and so has he," she said after a moment.

"Understood."

"I do have a guest room," Adler offered. "And there's an elevator."

"I'd expect nothing less." Morgan smiled down at her. There was a moment when Adler wondered what she was thinking. Her blue eyes lowered to Adler's lips. They reconnected with her eyes a moment later. "I'm going to get some sleep, okay? It's been a long day."

Adler nodded. She watched Morgan lie back down. Instead of rolling away to face the side of the tent as Brad had done, though, Morgan rolled to face Adler.

"Good night," Adler whispered.

"Night," Morgan whispered back. "Stay warm," she added.

CHAPTER 6

WHEN Morgan woke up, it was with her arm around Adler's waist. She slowly extricated herself from the other woman's body and pulled the sleeping bag away. The morning was chilly, but not unbearable. While Adler slept, she slid on her boots, unzipped the tent, and walked outside. She retrieved their food and other items from the bear container. It took only a few minutes to get a small fire started. Adler emerged from the tent looking adorable in her borrowed clothing. She'd put on her boots but hadn't tied them. She yawned and stretched as she stared up into the rising sun.

"I'm making coffee. I have granola bars," Morgan told her.

"Coffee?" Adler asked. "God, I'd love coffee."

"It's not a skim latte."

"I'm not that pretentious. I think you think I'm pretentious; I'm really not."

"Says the woman that didn't want to pee behind a tree," Morgan said with a laugh.

"I did it last night, didn't I?" Adler countered.

"That's true. I'm surprised you didn't hike all the way back to the bathrooms in the dark."

"I would have, but that would have left you without the lantern, and I wouldn't do that to you," Adler sat next to her on the log.

"Your phone has a flashlight."

"Shit. My phone," Adler said and stood.

"What's wrong?"

"We fell asleep. I put my phone on vibrate. I need to see if Brad called."

"Oh," Morgan replied. "I'll pour the coffee. We can pack up after we eat."

Adler walked briskly yet carefully back to the tent due to her shoes still not being tied. She zipped it up after a minute. Morgan could hear her talking through it but couldn't make out anything specific, until Adler raised her voice slightly. Then, she knew they were arguing. She felt both good and bad about that. She felt good because that meant they were having issues. That was a horrible thing to feel good about. She felt bad then, because she'd been the reason for the argument.

"Sorry about that," Adler said when she emerged. "He wasn't exactly happy."

"Sorry. It's my fault. Did you tell him that?"

"No, Morgan. None of this is your fault. If you don't mind, though, I think I'll skip the coffee and breakfast."

"Of course. We can get packed up."

"No, that's not–" Adler paused and sat back down next to Morgan. "I'm sorry. I don't want to ruin your last day here."

"It's okay. Come on."

***

"Brad, hey. You didn't need to meet me here."

"I just got back from picking up the rental car you left in town," he replied tersely.

Adler stood in front of him while Morgan sat in the driver's seat of her car. She turned to Morgan, not wanting this to be their goodbye, but not knowing how to avoid it when she needed to talk to her boyfriend and Morgan needed to finish packing to catch her flight. They were outside of her hotel. People were moving all around them. Brad was there. It all seemed too public somehow for a goodbye between the two of them.

"This is Morgan." Adler turned back to him and motioned to the woman behind her.

"Nice to meet you," Morgan said.

"You, too."

"Why are you wearing long underwear?" he asked, looking her up and down.

"Shit," she said under her breath and turned back to Morgan. "I can ship this stuff to you, or if you can wait, I can run into my room and change."

"You can keep it. It's fine. It kept you warm, right?" Morgan asked with a small smile.

"It did."

"Why did you need to be kept warm?" Brad asked.

"Brad, can you give me a minute?"

"Addie, I should go," Morgan said. "I should leave you two and–"

"Addie?" Brad asked.

"Brad, one second." Adler walked around to Morgan's side, resting her folded arms on the rolled-down window. "I'm sorry."

"It's okay."

"It's not. But I have to talk to him."

"I get it." Morgan shrugged. "Oh, I almost forgot." She reached down, pulled up something shiny, and handed it to Adler. "I found another one at this shop by one of the other places I was looking at for the store. I thought you'd like it."

"You should keep it," Adler said.

"I got one for myself." She held up another one. "Maybe, when you look at it, you'll think of me."

"I definitely will. Now, I have two."

Morgan smiled at her. Then, she looked ahead at the hotel parking lot.

"I should go."

"I'll call you," Adler said. "And thank you for last night, Morgan." She leaned in a little and pressed her lips to Morgan's cheek. "You were right: camping can be magical when you're with the right person," she whispered as she pulled away.

Morgan turned her face to Adler and said, "You can't say stuff like that to me."

"What? Why—"

"Have fun with your boyfriend. I hope you have a great rest of your trip." Morgan put the car in gear, gave Adler one final glance, and said, "Goodbye, Addie."

"Bye, Morgan."

Morgan drove off then, leaving Adler standing about ten feet away from the man she supposedly loved.

"She called you *Addie*. You hate being called *Addie*." Brad walked up to her. "And why did you need to be kept warm? You slept on her couch, Adler."

"Let's go inside, Brad."

"Why?"

"Because you're going to yell at me, and I don't want to be yelled at in public."

***

The argument was probably the worst they'd ever had, and they'd had a few good ones. Brad said some things he'd probably regret later, but they were well-deserved. Adler had lied to him. She'd told him she was sleeping on Morgan's coach when she'd really gone camping with someone who wasn't him. He'd taken that the hardest. They'd fallen asleep without actually finishing the argument, but both of them needed a break.

When she woke in the middle of the night to go to the bathroom, she'd gone to her suitcase where she'd placed both items Morgan had given to her. She looked at them for a long moment, thinking about how silly it was, before she tucked the pressed pennies back into the pocket. The first one, they'd found together in an outfitter's store Morgan was scoping out. They'd chosen a simple design, with Jackson Hole scrawled across the flattened penny in a beautiful script. The second one, the one Morgan had given her before she'd left, had been a different design. It was a tiny image of the Tetons themselves, with Grand Teton National Park written in even smaller letters. Morgan had gotten herself the same one. There was something special about her having an identical penny. There was something important about what she'd said before she'd left. Adler tried not to think about any of those things as she climbed into bed next to her slumbering boyfriend.

***

"I think it's just better if we go home," Brad said the following morning at breakfast. "This has been a train wreck. I get that some of that is my fault."

"Brad, it's my fault. I'm sorry. I should have just gone camping with you that first night."

"Then, why didn't you? Why is it that some stranger takes you camping and you're fine; but I want to do it, and it's a huge mistake?"

"It wasn't like that." Adler thought about lying to him again. She thought about telling him that Morgan and she had only planned on watching the sunset. They were going to leave after that, but something had happened, and they'd stayed. She knew that wouldn't work, though. She also knew she couldn't lie to him again. "Morgan asked. She does this stuff for a living. She owns a sports store and specializes in the outdoors. She was going to camp by herself and invited me."

"And you lied about that because?" He sipped his coffee.

"Because I knew it would upset you."

"Then, why did you do it, Adler?"

She swallowed hard and replied, "Because I wanted to spend more time with Morgan. It was her last night here."

He leaned back in his chair and seemed to calm before saying, "You really like her. I don't think I've ever seen you want to spend more time with someone, especially if that time was doing something you don't want to do. Paxton tried to get you to hang out with her girlfriend when they were still together."

"I had no desire to go sailing with them," she replied.

"But, with Morgan, you wanted to camp? Pax is your sister."

"I love my sister. I can see her whenever I want. We live ten minutes away from each other. I don't need to go sailing. I knew that girlfriend would be an ex one day. I didn't need to spend any more time with her."

"What do you want to do, babe? Do you want to stay here for the rest of our vacation? Do you want to just go home? Go somewhere else?"

The answer that came to mind first was that she wanted to spend more time with Morgan. She wished she hadn't left. If Morgan were still in Jackson Hole, Adler would've stayed here. Without her, though, it just didn't seem worth it. She would examine what that meant later. She looked over at her dutiful boyfriend, who'd planned this trip for them. It wasn't what she'd wanted, but he'd tried. Part of her wanted to say that they should stay. They could spend the rest of their time together exploring the town and going on a few hikes here and there. They could have nice meals together and make love every night. They were supposed to be celebrating their love, after all. They'd yet to touch each other beyond a kiss hello or goodbye since they'd arrived. The other part of her wanted to go home. She felt the need to wallow. It was strange. She took a long drink of her coffee and wondered why it felt like she'd just gotten her heart broken, when the man who loved her was sitting right in front of her, asking her what she wanted to do.

Adler had woken the previous morning in a tent, with Morgan's arm draped over her waist. She'd pretended to still be asleep for several minutes before Morgan slid out of the tent. The long-sleeved shirt she'd borrowed had ridden up slightly in the night. Morgan's hand was mostly touching the fabric, but there had been a finger or two that had brushed against Adler's skin. It lit her up like a fire she hadn't been prepared for. She didn't know whether she should stoke it to make the fire grow or dump some cold water on it and put it out. She did know, though. She knew she needed to put it out. It made no sense. She had this handsome man sitting in front of her that was only trying to make her happy, even though she'd been a terrible girlfriend.

"Let's just go home."

CHAPTER 7

"WHEN was the last time you talked to her?" Kinsley asked.

"A few days ago," Morgan said, using the chopsticks to snag a shrimp from Kinsley's plate. "Where'd all the shrimp go? There's only one left."

"Riley ate them," Kinsley replied.

"I did. Sue me." Riley held her chopsticks in the air.

"Have I told you how inconvenient it is that your girlfriend and I like the same Chinese food?" Morgan asked with a roll of her eyes in Riley's direction followed by a smile.

"I told you to order more," Riley said to Kinsley.

"You also told me you'd be working late," Kinsley said back to her. "And *you* didn't tell me you'd eat more than an army," she told Morgan.

"I resent that," Morgan said. "And resemble it."

"I cooked enough for two people," Kinsley said.

"I came home early. Would you have preferred me to stay at work all night?" Riley asked. "I finished the affidavit I was working on faster than I thought."

"I'm glad you're home. Just share with my friend Morgan, who is, apparently, starving." Kinsley leaned over and kissed Riley's cheek.

"I didn't eat all day. I was working and kind of forgot."

"You didn't forget to text Adler, though, and arrange a FaceTime call for tomorrow," Kinsley reminded.

"FaceTime?" Riley asked.

"Addie texted me. We do that sometimes," Morgan said with a shrug.

"How often is *sometimes*?" Riley asked, taking a sip of her red wine.

"I don't know. It's a few times a day. Sometimes, more. Sometimes, less."

They sat at Kinsley and Riley's dining room table, eating the amazing food Kinsley had prepared for them. Well, she'd prepared it for herself and Morgan.

Morgan liked Riley as a person. She loved her for Kinsley, who had been so happy since they'd started dating; even more so since Riley had moved into her house. Morgan also just wanted a night with her closest friend. She'd watched it happen twice now. First, Reese, her ex-girlfriend and best friend in the world, met and fell for Kellan. Slowly, Morgan had been replaced as Reese's person. It made sense. Morgan liked Kellan, too. Gradually, though, there was less and less time for Reese and Morgan that didn't involve Kellan, too.

Morgan and Kinsley had always been close. But once Reese and Kellan got together, the two single women of their friend group started spending more time together. Before Morgan knew it, Kinsley had become her closest friend and the one she revealed all her secrets to. Then, Kinsley and Riley reconnected. Once they'd started dating, it had been difficult for Morgan to get any of Kinsley's time. Now that the couple was more settled, things had evened out. But Morgan really just wanted her friend tonight.

"And she's not your girlfriend?" Riley asked, running her fingers along Kinsley's forearm, which rested atop the table.

"She's a friend, Riley. She's straight and has a boyfriend."

"Sorry. It's just confusing. You kind of act how most couples act. I have friends I don't talk to for weeks or months. We definitely don't text every day," Riley replied.

"Yeah, look at us, Morgan." Kinsley took a drink and continued, "Sometimes, I go days without talking to you and weeks without seeing you. We both get so busy. From what you've told me, Adler is a workaholic."

"She is."

"She's finding a lot of time to talk to you, though."

"She's a friend, and we live in different places. It's kind of all we can do, James," Morgan said to her friend.

"And you have no feelings for her at all?" Kinsley asked.

"James…"

"Morgan, it's been over a month since you got back." Kinsley took Riley's hand. "Other than work, this woman is all I've heard you talk about."

"She's my new friend. My old friends have been coupling off, lately. I made a new one. Don't give me a hard time about this." Morgan finished her wine.

"Fine. I just don't want you to get hurt."

"Neither do I," Riley replied.

"I don't want myself to get hurt, either," Morgan admitted softly to herself.

***

It had been five weeks since Morgan had seen Adler Williams in Jackson Hole. She hated to admit to herself that she'd waited for Adler's first phone call, but she had. It had been three days after she'd returned to South Lake. Adler had texted first. They'd exchanged a few messages before she'd called Morgan. They'd spoken for over an hour. The next day, the texting had begun in full force. They weren't texting good mornings or good nights to each other, but nearly everything in between.

"Hey. I thought we were doing FaceTime. I have my iPad at just the right angle so that I don't look like I have a double chin," Morgan said into her phone.

"I know. I'm sorry. I just called to tell you that I have to postpone."

"Work?" Morgan asked.

"Yes. It's a last-minute meeting with the board. We

had some issues with a massive shipment of cheese that needs to be recalled now."

"Ah, the cheese recall. Yes, I understand," Morgan replied sarcastically.

"Food distribution at its finest. I am sorry, though."

"It's fine. I understand. I have always had more work than I have time for, anyway," Morgan said.

"You're really okay with me canceling?" Adler asked.

"You said *postponing*. That implies we'll do it sometime in the future. Canceling means we won't do it at all."

"Sorry, I meant *postponing*." Adler laughed lightly.

Morgan allowed herself a moment to listen and said, "Yes, I'm fine with it. I get it. You're in charge of a lot of people, places, and things. That takes time to manage. These things happen. Can we maybe do it tomorrow? I'm going camping for the weekend with James, Riley, Reese, Kellan, and this woman Riley knows from her old law office in North Lake after that. Her name is Laura or Leslie, I think. I don't know. I only heard that she was coming yesterday."

Morgan had mentioned her friends to Adler on numerous occasions. She knew James was Kinsley James, that she and Riley were a couple, and that Reese was her ex-girlfriend who was engaged to Kellan.

"Laura or Leslie?"

"Yeah, she's just here for the weekend. Riley invited her to come along. I guess she's a big rock climber and wants to check out a spot here she's never climbed before."

There was a moment of silence before Adler said, "I'm sure you guys will have a great time. How far is North Lake from where you live?"

"Huh?" Morgan asked, confused by the relevance of the question. "Oh, it depends on the time of year. It's a little over seventy miles all the way around. She lives in Truckee, where Riley used to live. It's basically right at the top, and I'm right at the bottom. When tourists are here in the summer, it can sometimes take over an hour to get there. In the winter, the weather is the problem. Why?"

"Just curious," Adler said. "I have to go, though. The meeting is starting in five minutes. How about tomorrow night, we FaceTime? Around eight?"

"As long as you don't mind me packing while we talk, that sounds good."

"I don't mind."

"I'll talk to you then," Morgan said.

"Hey, Morgan?" Adler asked.

"Yeah?"

Adler sighed and said, "I miss you. Is that weird to say?"

"No." Morgan sighed back. "It's not weird. I miss you, too."

"I've got to go. Tomorrow?"

"Tomorrow."

***

"Hey, are you ready for dinner?" Brad asked when he entered Adler's apartment using his key.

"Dinner?" She looked up from the laptop she'd stationed at her kitchen table. She looked over at the pasta she'd reheated from the lunch she hadn't eaten earlier that day. "Did we have a dinner planned tonight?"

"No. We just talked about maybe doing something this week." He stood in front of the table, tossing his car keys back and forth. "I feel like I haven't seen you in forever, with the project starting up and your work. I thought I'd stop by."

"But you just asked if I was ready for dinner as if we'd planned something specific," Adler countered.

"It was just an expression, Adler. It's dinner time. I thought you might be interested in having some with me," he replied. "But I can see you already ate." He nodded toward the bowl of pasta.

"I kind of planned to talk to Morgan tonight. We're going to FaceTime at eight. I wanted to eat and get a little work done before then," she told him.

"Morgan?"

"Yeah, Morgan."

"You talk to Morgan every day," he said as he sat in the empty chair next to her.

"I know. I talk to you every day, too, Brad."

"I'm your boyfriend, Adler," he replied.

"Morgan is my friend. I'm not allowed to talk to my friends every day if I want?" she asked, pushing the pasta bowl away for no reason in particular.

"Babe, since I started this project, I've had less time for us. I'm here now. Can't we go grab a nice dinner, have some wine, come back here, and spend the rest of the night together?" he asked.

"I just ate, Brad." She looked down at her computer. "It's like three minutes before eight. How about I FaceTime with Morgan, since I already postponed with her once? I can meet you at your place later."

"Why can't I just stay here and watch TV or something while you talk to her?" he asked a completely reasonable question.

"I don't know. I like to talk to her in private."

"I wouldn't interfere with your conversation, Adler. I can even go watch TV in the bedroom," he replied.

"I just wish you would have called first," she said before she'd thought about it. "That's not–"

"No, you're right." Brad stood, clearly not meaning what he'd just said. "I should have called. I should have warned my girlfriend that I wanted to take her to a nice dinner instead of using the key she'd given me to her place six months ago. I should have checked her calendar to see if she was FaceTiming with the random woman she met on that God-awful trip I planned for her, that got ruined in part because of that random woman."

"Hey! Don't take out our issues on Morgan. She didn't have anything to do with you randomly deciding to take me to the middle of nowhere, Brad," she argued.

"Yet, you had no problem going with *her* to the middle of nowhere," he argued back.

"I wanted to go with her." Adler stood. "I wanted to go with her, Brad. I was having a nice time with her, and she suggested we go out to see this view. It was gorgeous, and I loved it. She wanted to stay, and I said yes. I have apologized for lying to you about it. I've apologized for wanting to go with her and not with you, but I did want to go with her that night."

"What does that even mean, Adler?" he asked, running both hands through his mussed hair after a long day at the worksite.

"I didn't want to go camping with you, Brad."

"That part I understand."

"I don't think I wanted to go on an anniversary trip with you, either," she said softly.

"No, I got that, too." He lowered his head. "Can you just say it, so I'll finally know?"

She sighed and replied, "I think we should break up."

CHAPTER 8

"HEY. Is everything okay?" Morgan asked at 8:15, when Adler called her back. "I thought we were going to FaceTime at eight. Work?"

"Not exactly," Adler replied. "Can we just talk on the phone tonight?"

Morgan could detect something in Adler's tone that normally wasn't present in their conversations about their respective days, friends, and significant others in Adler's situation. She sat on the end of the bed, clutching a pair of shorts in one hand and her phone in the other.

"What's going on?" she asked, stuffing the shorts into her pack.

"I wanted to apologize for being late. I didn't plan on messing this up again," Adler said.

"Addie, what are you talking about?" Morgan chuckled lightly. "It's a phone call. I get that you're busy. You always let me know when you can or can't talk."

"How is it that *you* understand how busy I am and that sometimes I might be late, but Brad doesn't?"

Morgan knew then what was going on. Brad must have made another comment about Adler working all the time. He'd done that a few times since Morgan had known her. Adler, in Morgan's opinion, really did do her best to balance everything. She tried to leave the office by six at the latest. Morgan knew that because she usually texted her that she was finally heading home for the day. She usually had one night a week that she reserved for Brad. Sometimes, he was too busy, and *he* had to cancel. It wasn't perfect, but it was Addie. This was the life she wanted for herself.

"What happened?" Morgan asked as she stood, moved to the bathroom, and grabbed her toiletry bag.

"We broke up."

Morgan stopped immediately. Her eyes were on the floor. In that moment, something changed within her. It wasn't something good, either. Adler Williams was single. Brad was out of the picture. Morgan could ask her out. No, she couldn't. Adler was single, but she was also straight. Morgan swallowed hard, tossed her zipped toiletry bag onto her bed, and walked to the dresser to remove the rest of the clothes she'd need for her weekend.

"I'm sorry, Addie."

"You should be. It's all your fault," Adler replied, but she was laughing.

"What's that mean?" Morgan laughed back, hiding her concern.

"He was jealous of you."

Morgan flopped onto the bed again and asked, "Me? Why?" She gulped, lowered the phone for a moment, and put it back to her ear.

"I spend too much time talking to you and not enough of my time with him; which I understand. I know why it made him upset, I do. I just didn't know how to solve the problem."

"Probably talk to me less," Morgan replied and promptly squished her eyes together while she shook her head.

"I don't want to do that," Adler said softly. "I think it came down to something that says a lot about my relationship with him. The little time I have leftover for people in my life, I didn't want him to fill it. I know that's bad. He's—" Adler stopped herself. "He *was* my boyfriend. Past tense." She paused on a sigh. "I have two people I want to spend more time with than my long-term boyfriend. One is my sister, Pax. The other one is you."

"I'm honored." Morgan shook her head again. "Idiot," she whispered.

"What?"

"Nothing," she replied too quickly.

"He took what little stuff he'd left here when he went home. He even left his key. It's for the best, I think, though. I didn't love him. I'm not sure if I ever did. I probably did, though, right? I was with him for over a year."

"I think that's a question you need to answer for yourself, Addie."

"That's another thing he was mad about," Adler replied. "You call me that."

"Addie? Should I not call you that? You never said I-"

"Historically, I have not liked that nickname, no. I don't even let Paxton call me that. Brad was no exception to that rule."

"But I am?" she asked with a smile.

"I like how it sounds when you say it," Adler replied.

Morgan's phone beeped at her. She pulled it away from her ear to see that James was calling.

"Hey, can you hang on one second?" she asked Adler.

"Oh, shit. You're packing tonight, aren't you?"

"I am, but it's not that. James is calling. She's picking me up tomorrow morning. I should answer," she replied.

"I should just let you go. I know you have a busy weekend with your friends."

"Adler, you just broke up with your boyfriend. Give me a minute to talk to James, and I'll be right back. We can talk as long as you need to."

"No, it's fine. Surprisingly, I'm not heartbroken over the whole thing. I don't even think he was that heartbroken, either. We both said it was over. He grabbed his stuff and left."

Her phone beeped, and she said, "Addie, one sec, okay?"

"Can you just call me when you get back? I think I want to have a bath and a glass of wine before I go to bed."

"Okay. Sure. I'll call you Sunday night."

"Have fun, Morgan."

"Night, Addie." Morgan clicked over to James. "This better be good."

***

The drive to their hiking trail took only about forty minutes. By the end of it, though, Morgan was sure of exactly two things. She no longer wanted to go camping with her friends, and this was a total set up. Laura was a nice girl. She was about two years older than Morgan. She was a lawyer that had recently made partner in her firm. She was an avid fan of the outdoors, including her favored activity of rock climbing, which she talked non-stop about the entire ride in James' car. It was the six of them. Riley and Kinsley were in the front, with Kinsley behind the wheel. Kellan and Reese were in the middle. That left the back seat for Morgan and Laura. It was a seat made for three people, but Laura didn't seem to like personal space. Morgan had figured that out about ten minutes into the drive. She'd placed her pack between them, pretending to need something from it, and then leaving it there as a hint.

"I heard you're a great kayaker," Laura said as they hiked.

"I'm okay. Who told you I was great?" Morgan asked.

"Riley."

"I'm not sure how exactly Riles would know I'm a great kayaker," she said loudly to get Riley's attention from her place about ten feet ahead on the trail.

"Maybe we could go out on the water sometime," Laura suggested.

"Maybe," Morgan replied, hoping the subject would change. Then, she saw the clearing ahead. "I think we're at the site."

Morgan marched a little faster, passing her friends, until she was in front of all of them. She turned to face them, giving them her most frustrated glare.

"Really?" she whispered.

"What?" James asked.

"Laura, that's what."

They made their way into the clearing. Morgan kept

walking until she was near the fire pit. Then, she tossed her gear down and pulled on Kinsley's arm. Kinsley's other arm was attached to her girlfriend's. Riley came with them. While Reese, seeming to understand Morgan's plight, occupied Laura with conversation.

"Are you kidding me?" Morgan asked.

"What? She's nice," Riley replied.

"Nice *and* chatty," Morgan countered. "She didn't shut up the entire way here. She kept asking me about my preferred climbing technique. Did you know that some climbers are slow and deliberate, with a static technique? Some climbers use a fast, dynamic climbing technique. I do now."

"Morgan, she's excited. She'll calm down now that we're here," Kinsley said.

"Why is she so excited? Did she know you two, idiots, were setting us up?" Morgan pointed between the two of them. "You failed to mention that to me."

"She's recently out of a relationship. Well, not recently; they broke up last year. But she's ready to start dating again. She loves the outdoors. You love the outdoors. She's a successful businesswoman. You're a successful business-woman. Kinsley and I thought you two should meet," Riley said.

"I am also a Pisces. Is she a Pisces?"

"I don't know," Riley replied. "I can–"

"No, I don't need you to check," Morgan interrupted. "Guys, I'm not interested in meeting anyone right now. Things at work are–"

"So busy," Kinsley interrupted. "We know. They always are. When are you going to meet someone if you're always working?"

"And don't say you don't want to meet someone, because Kinsley and I have both listened to you talk about how you want to find someone," Riley added.

"Not Laura." Morgan nodded behind her.

"You could give her a chance. I mean, you guys are sharing a tent tonight," Kinsley replied.

"Damn, I hadn't thought about that."

"Maybe if you find someone, you'll share a tent with them, and you won't be the single girl needing to share a tent with the other single girl," Kinsley suggested.

"You guys really suck sometimes," she replied.

She turned to go, but Kinsley took her arm and turned her back to herself. She looked at her girlfriend, who took the hint and walked toward the other women.

"Morgan, I'm sorry. I honestly thought you'd get along with her. She's excitable, but she's also kind and funny. She's smart, too. She's also easy on the eyes." She nodded toward the dark-haired woman. "You've just been spending all your free time talking to a certain unavailable woman. Riles and I wanted you to, maybe, meet someone who was available."

"For your information, Adler broke up with her boyfriend. She is available now."

"Oh, Morgan... No, she's not. She's still straight," Kinsley reminded.

***

"Can I ask you a question?" Laura shifted in her sleeping bag.

"Sure," Morgan replied reluctantly.

"You're not interested in me at all, are you?"

Morgan turned her head to face the woman lying next to her, but there was no light in the tent. She couldn't make out Laura's features to tell if she was upset by this or just asking the question to know the answer.

"It's not you."

"Please don't say *it's not you, it's me*," Laura replied with a soft laugh.

"No, that's not what I was going to say. My friends decided to set me up without my consent. I wasn't really looking to meet anyone on this trip. It was just supposed to be all of us hanging out, which we hadn't done in a while."

"Then, Riley invited me along and ruined it for you," she said.

"Not ruined it, Laura. I just wasn't expecting to be thrust into a blind date while hiking and then have to share a tent with someone I don't even know," she replied.

"I'm sorry. I honestly thought they'd told you. Riley mentioned to me that you'd be here and that you're single. She didn't come out and say, 'Blind date,' specifically. But it was implied. I didn't realize they hadn't done the same with you." She paused to exhale deeply. "I come on a little strong sometimes," Laura said. "I was in a very long relationship. We weren't legally married, but we were in every other way. We were together for fourteen years. I thought we'd be together forever. A year ago, it ended. This is technically my first foray back into the dating world, and I realize I may have talked your ear off about rock climbing and my love of the outdoors. The only thing I knew about you, beyond that you were single and gay, was that you liked the same stuff I do."

"Our friends didn't handle this very well, did they?" Morgan asked into the darkness.

"No, I guess not." Laura chuckled. "Is there any way we can, maybe, start over? I'd still like to get to know you and have you get to know me, if you're up for it."

"I'd like to get to know you, but I think I'd like to do that as a friend, if that's okay."

"I really did put you off, huh?" the woman asked playfully.

"It really isn't you. That's not a line or my way of trying to get you to back down. I'm just not in a place where I want to date."

"Because?" the woman asked. "If you don't mind me asking."

"Because there is something very wrong with me," Morgan answered.

"How so?"

"I'm in love with a straight girl," Morgan said.

CHAPTER 9

"WE'RE both young and single," Paxton said.

"Well, we're youngish and single," Adler replied, clinking their wineglasses together.

"Better than old spinsters."

"That's true, I guess." Adler looked down at her phone, which hadn't rung or buzzed with a text in more than a day. "Want another?" she asked her sister.

"Two is my limit tonight. I'm driving," Paxton replied. "Why do you keep checking your phone?"

"I don't."

"Yes, you do. It's Sunday. I know you work a lot, but who's emailing you on a Sunday night?"

"No one. Morgan's just been on a camping trip. I'm used to hearing from her."

"Morgan, huh?"

"I've mentioned Morgan to you," Adler replied, taking the last sip from her wine. "I'm getting the check."

She waved over the bartender, who quickly printed their receipt, dropped it on the bar, and moved on to the next customer.

"You've *only* mentioned Morgan to me," Paxton said. "I don't think I've heard you talk about Brad for weeks. You don't seem broken up at all about you guys ending things."

"It was a long time coming." Adler turned to her sister, dropping her credit card on top of the check. "And what do you mean I *only* talk about Morgan?"

"I mean that if I didn't know you were straight, big sis, I would think you were totally into this Morgan girl."

"She's my friend. She's one of my only friends."

"Because you're too busy to make them," Paxton replied.

"Yes. But now that Brad and I are done, I'll have more time." Adler signed the returned credit card receipt. "Are you ready?"

"I'm ready." Paxton stood from the tall bar stool. "I'm just saying… You spent more time on the phone and texting with Morgan than you probably did in person with your boyfriend, Adler."

"Brad and I weren't working." Adler stood up next to her sister. "And work is going really well lately. I was able to hire those two additional directors I wanted, which means I'll have less I have to do every day."

"And now that you have extra time, since you're single and you have less work to do, what are you going to do with it?" Paxton asked as they walked out of their favorite bar.

"I don't know. Maybe I'll pick up a hobby."

Paxton laughed loudly and replied, "You are *not* a hobby kind of girl."

"I could be a hobby kind of a girl," Adler argued as she held open the door for her sister and followed her out.

"Okay. Give me an example of a hobby you could take up," Paxton replied.

Adler considered for a moment before she replied, "I'm starting to think I could get into the outdoors."

***

Adler had just pulled the blanket up to cover herself when her phone buzzed on her bedside table. Before it had even finished its notification, she'd picked it up to see that it was a text from Morgan. She didn't want to appear too eager, so she waited a full minute before she dialed Morgan's number and put the phone to her ear.

"Hey, camper." She smacked her own forehead immediately.

"Camper, huh?" Morgan asked. "Sorry, I know it's kind of late. We just got back. I hope I didn't wake you."

"No. I went out with my sister tonight. I just got home a few minutes ago." It wasn't a total lie. She'd gotten home about an hour before. She'd taken a long bath, had another glass of wine, and climbed into bed. "How was your trip?"

"It was awkward. Then, it was good. Then, I was ready to come home. I have a ton of unpacking and some laundry to do, but that can wait until tomorrow when I get home from work."

"Why was it awkward?" Adler asked, settling into her pillow.

"Oh, Riley and Kinsley thought it would be fun to set me up with that friend they invited."

"Set you up? Like, a date?"

"A camping blind date, to be exact," Morgan replied.

"Oh." Adler thought for a moment about what to say next. "You said it was awkward and then it was good. What happened?"

"Laura really is a badass rock climber. When we got to the place she wanted to climb on Saturday, she rocked it. She actually climbed back down and helped the rest of us make it to the top. Well, it was an easier part of the climb, but we all made it up. Then, we had lunch at the top. There was this amazing view. It was peaceful. We had a lot of fun. There was a trail down the back. We hiked for a few hours until we got back to the car."

"And what about the blind date part?" Adler asked.

"My friends are idiots. I mean, Reese and Kellan, obviously, shared a tent. Riley and Kinsley did, too. That left the other two-person tent for the total strangers they thought would make a good couple. It was awkward that first night, but Saturday was so much fun. After dinner, Laura and I just talked in the tent. I'm pretty sure we heard Riles and James having sex, but I'm pretending it was bears mating in the woods, because I don't want to bleach my ears."

Adler laughed and replied, "God, I heard my sister and one of her exes have sex once, when we all went on spring break. Never get an adjoining hotel room with your sister when there's a chance the bed will share a wall."

"That's a good piece of advice, I guess." Morgan sighed. "My body is screaming. I think I need to take a bath and go to bed. I have payroll tomorrow morning and inventory after that."

"Hey, Morgan?"

"Yeah?"

"I was thinking about maybe coming to Tahoe."

"You were?" Morgan asked, sounding a little more awake suddenly.

Adler smiled and replied, "My last vacation was kind of a bust."

"How are you? It's been a few days since the Brad thing."

"I'm doing well. Thanks for worrying about me."

"Always," Morgan replied thoughtfully. "Are you really thinking of visiting?"

"Is there a chance I could see you if I do?"

"You're staying with me, Adler. I'd hope you see me."

"I don't have–"

"Yes, you do." Morgan paused for a moment. "You know I've only lived in this house for, like, three months. It's not anywhere near how I want it to be, but Kinsley was able to find it for me. It's got two extra bedrooms. One of them is actually ready for a guest. It belongs to you whenever you want it."

"Do you have any more camping trips coming up I should keep in mind?"

"Only if you're going, Addie."

"Okay," Adler replied with a shy smile and a slight

blush she was glad Morgan couldn't see. "Can you take me somewhere in Tahoe that's special to you?"

"I'll take you wherever you want, Addie," Morgan said softly. "When can you come?"

"Let me look at my calendar and see when I can get away. Can I text you tomorrow?"

"Tomorrow, yes. That's fine," Morgan replied.

"I'll let you get some sleep. Good night, Morgan," Adler said.

"Night, Addie."

***

Adler checked her calendar the following morning while sitting at her desk in her abnormally large office. The other furniture around her only made the space appear more desolate. There was a round table that fit four chairs. Next to that was a small, two-person sofa. On the other wall were a bookshelf and a window that had a beautiful view she never took in. Her desk was modern, but still just as large as those old wood desks. She had two guest chairs in front of it. There was one plant resting atop a small table below the window. The only reason the plant was still alive was because her assistant watered it for her.

She stared at the sometimes overlapping appointments on her calendar, wondering how she'd be able to pull off leaving for even a few days. Then, she thought back to how excited Morgan had sounded at the prospect of her visiting and made a decision.

"Matt, can you come in here for a minute?" she asked through the intercom on her phone.

Her assistant, Matt, walked into her office and said, "Want me to order lunch?"

"No. Can you put a meeting on my calendar for all the directors for sometime today?"

"What's the priority?"

"Have them move whatever they need to," she replied.

"And the topic?"

"Delegation," she said.

***

"Why are you obsessing?" James asked her.

"I am not obsessing," Morgan replied. "I'm cleaning. There's a difference."

Morgan wiped at the dresser she'd already dusted at least three times since Adler had confirmed the dates she'd be visiting. She'd also washed the bed linens twice, just to be sure they still had that freshly laundered scent. She'd placed candles around the room to give it a comfortable vibe. She'd also turned the guest bathroom into a hotel by ensuring she had tiny shampoo and conditioner bottles, bath wash, lotion, toothpaste, and even a travel toothbrush. Of course, Adler would bring all those things with her. Morgan just wanted her to feel as at home as possible.

"Morgan, you've laid out three layers of guest towels. *Layers*," she emphasized the word. "You have a huge towel and a medium towel and then a smaller towel above it."

"That's how you do guest towels," Morgan replied, grabbing her dust rag and heading out of the guest room.

"Morgan, you're not getting your hopes up, are you?" James asked as she followed her out and down the stairs.

"Hopes about what?"

"Has she at all expressed any inclination toward the female form?"

"Are you asking me if she's told me she finds a woman hot?" Morgan asked from the bottom of the steps.

"I'm just trying to figure out if you're head over heels for a woman you spent a few days in person with. As far as you know, she's straight and not interested in dating any woman."

"Your concern, my dear friend Kinsley, is noted," she replied.

"What are you guys going to do when she gets here?"

"Hang out," Morgan answered with a shrug.

They entered her kitchen, which she'd also cleaned from top to bottom and then top to bottom again. Morgan wiped a rogue stain on the kitchen island. Kinsley sat at the kitchen table.

"Hang out doing what?"

"I don't know, James. We'll do whatever we want. Now, will you go home so I can pick her up at the airport? Her flight arrives in an hour. Don't you have a girlfriend to annoy?"

"My girlfriend is busy," Kinsley replied. "But I will leave you alone. You're always like this when you have a crush."

"No, I'm not." Morgan squinted her eyes at her friend. "And I don't have a crush."

CHAPTER 10

W HEN Adler walked out of the airport, dragging her roller bag behind her with her overly large backpack over both shoulders, she wondered for a moment if she was crazy for doing this. She'd just taken another two weeks off from her COO job. Granted, her previous vacation ended up only being a few days. She'd delegated everything she could to her team. She also knew she'd check emails and would be fairly responsive whenever she could. She'd just traveled to a place she'd never been, to visit someone she'd spent only a few days with nearly two months ago. As she stood on the sidewalk, looking around for Morgan's red SUV, she considered her sister's comment at the bar that night. Was there something more happening between them than just friendship? Would she even be interested in that if Morgan wanted to pursue it?

"Addie," Morgan half-yelled from across the lanes of cars moving to drop off and pick up passengers.

"Hey," Adler yelled and waved so rapidly back and forth at her, she could feel the breeze from her arm. "Idiot," she whispered to herself.

"I'm in short-term parking," Morgan yelled, hooking a thumb behind her.

"I'll come to you."

Adler waited until there was a break in the traffic. She hefted her backpack and grabbed her roller. She made her way across the lanes to the other side, where Morgan greeted her with a wide smile, gorgeous and bright eyes, and a bouquet of flowers.

"I would have been here sooner, but I wanted to stop for these." The woman held them out in between them.

"You didn't have to get me flowers," Adler replied, wondering if this was something friends did for each other when they picked them up at airports. She'd only ever had boyfriends get her flowers when she'd needed a ride. "But, thank you. This is very sweet."

"You're welcome." Morgan met Adler's eyes before turning her head slightly. "Is that a backpack?"

"It's the one you recommended I buy for camping."

"You bought a camping pack?" Morgan asked with an ever-widening smile.

"I'm here for two weeks. I thought we could, maybe, go over the weekend or something," Adler replied.

Morgan looked good. Were her legs always that shapely in the shorts she'd worn in Jackson Hole? They looked long, soft, and athletically muscled. Her hair was pulled back, giving Adler a perfect view of her round but not too round face, bright blue eyes, and delicious-looking mouth. Did she just call Morgan's mouth *delicious*?

"We could go tomorrow if you want. I'd just need to pack and pick up some staples from the store for however long we'll be. Did you like that chicken we had? I can make that again and show you how to do the prep in the kitchen."

"Tomorrow's Monday," Adler replied.

"I took the week off. Well, I have a few things I need to do, but I wanted to spend as much time with you as possible while you're here. I'll check in when I need to, and if everything is okay, I'll take some time off next week, too."

They started walking into the parking lot, with Morgan taking the handle of Adler's roller bag from her.

"You didn't have to do that," Adler said. "Were you worried about me rummaging through your stuff when you're not around or something?"

"Yes, Adler. That was what I was thinking when I took time off to hang out with my friend." Morgan chuckled. "This is me."

They climbed into the car after loading Adler's stuff into the back. Morgan pulled out of the lot and onto the road. The music on the radio was contemporary pop, which somehow suited Morgan Burns. The weather was cool, but not cold. Their windows were down. The breeze was running through the hair Adler had down. She inhaled the fresh scent of the pure air around her. She'd been in Tahoe for all of ten minutes, and she was already in love. She just wasn't sure if it was with the scenery outside the window or the woman currently tapping her fingers on her steering wheel, sitting next to her.

***

"I thought you said this place wasn't done," Adler said after Morgan had given her the tour.

"It's not," Morgan replied, pouring them each a glass of white wine. "I want to start on the backyard, since it's still nice outside. James is going to help. We can do most of it ourselves. I want a real deck out there, with a grill and furniture. The yard is small, but it's doable." She paused to pass Adler the glass. "And I need furniture for the other bedroom. I want to redo the tile in here. The list is endless."

"The place is beautiful, Morgan. You've already done so much in just a few months. Do you ever stop?" Adler chuckled and took a sip of the cold, sweet wine. "I mean, you work at work, and then you work at home, and then you work *on* your home."

"Says the COO." Morgan took a drink and sat down at the table next to her. "I'm glad you're here, Addie."

"So am I." Adler lifted her glass in a toast. "To us and my first trip to Tahoe," she said.

Morgan lifted her glass and replied, "To us."

The smile she gave Adler in that moment conveyed all Adler needed to know.

***

"When are we going to get to meet her, then?" James asked.

"I don't know. When we get back," Morgan replied into her phone. "James, we're only going for a couple of days. Well, maybe a few. I don't know. I just told Jake, over at the campground, to give me the best yurt he had at the last minute over at Fallen Leaf."

"You're not going somewhere with a lake view?" James asked.

"No, Fallen Leaf Campground is much more private and away from all the tourists. I figured we'd take the Moraine Trail one day. It's short. We can hit up the Fallen Leaf Lake beach instead of Pope or Baldwin, which are always packed this time of year."

"Looking for privacy, huh?" James asked.

"I've got to go. She's coming out."

"She is, is she?" James laughed.

"Shut up. Bye." Morgan hung up the phone. "Are you all set?" she asked Adler, who'd emerged from the house, walking to the SUV. "Everything's in the car."

"I'm good. I just wanted to use the modern facilities one more time," Adler replied with a wink.

"Well, the place I'm taking you to has bathrooms. It also has showers. You pay for them in coins, but I brought a bunch."

"Somehow, you already know me so well." Adler laughed. She opened the driver's side door and said, "For you."

"Thank you," Morgan said with a laugh and climbed into the car.

Adler closed the door and walked to the other side. She climbed in next to Morgan.

"I think you'll like this place. It's not a five-star resort, but it's a combination of pure camping with a little bit of modernity," Morgan explained.

"I like it so far," Adler replied.

They drove the short distance to the Fallen Leaf Campground, which was situated on the north shore of the Fallen Leaf Lake. The campground featured hundreds of campsites. It also had six yurts or cabin-like structures. Morgan knew the camp host, Jake, well. They worked together to coordinate tours and other packages for the guests. He'd been able to secure her a yurt at the last minute thanks to a cancelation. Each yurt provided a cabin-like space for a family of five or six. It would work very well for just the two of them. They'd also have a bear-proof food storage locker, campfire ring, pedestal grill, and a picnic table.

The yurts sat on a wooden platform and actually had one electric light and a space heater they'd likely not need. There weren't many other signs of modernity in the place. Each yurt also had a futon and bunk beds with mattresses. Morgan had chosen a yurt instead of a tent for that reason. One of them could sleep on the futon. One could take a bunk. Both of them could take bunks, and they could use the futon for sitting or to put their stuff on it. Either way, it left space between them that Morgan would likely need when they fell asleep.

The site did not offer views of the lake, but they were nestled among towering pine, cedar, fir, and aspen trees. The one Jake had scored for her was even adjacent to a wild-flower meadow. Fallen Leaf Lake was nearby. It was where the forested shoreline and surrounding mountains were reflected in its crystal blue water.

"Morgan, this is beautiful," Adler said as they climbed out of the car.

"You haven't seen the inside yet. I don't think you'd call it beautiful, but it's probably better than being on the ground in a tiny tent."

Adler turned to her and said, "You know I'd happily share a tent with you, though, right?"

"I figured you're still getting used to being a camper. This was a good warm-up."

"Laura's a big-time camper, though, huh?" Adler asked as she hefted her pack from the back of the car.

"Who?" Morgan asked, placing the cooler on the ground. "Oh, Laura! I guess."

Morgan watched Adler smile. She wondered what that was about, but she also wanted to get all their things inside and get everything set up for the night. She'd worry about that smile later. They carried all their belongings inside the small structure. To the left was the futon, which was still in its sofa form. To the right were the bunk beds. That was the extent of the furniture in the room. It was basic, but it would work.

"Not beautiful, but still nice," Adler said and dropped her backpack onto the floor.

"Better than a tent?"

"I think *you* think I don't want to share a tent with you. Morgan, I really wouldn't mind." Adler's cheeks blushed then.

That was when Morgan knew. She smiled back. She was certain her own cheeks were a shade of crimson. She dropped her own bag to the floor, bent down, and pulled out a small bag.

"I actually got you something," Morgan said as she stood. "Here."

She passed the small, brown paper bag to Adler, who looked at it curiously. Then, she must have felt what was inside. She smiled, opened it, and dumped out its contents into her hand.

"Pressed pennies." She chuckled.

"I drive from store to store sometimes. I found these from all around. I figured you could start a real collection. Silly, I know, but–"

"Just wait," Adler interrupted. She bent down and searched inside her own bag. "Look." She held up a small black, flat object. On the front it said, *'Penny Passport.'* "I got this for the ones you gave me. I haven't added any new ones to it, but I got you one of these, too. I thought you could add new ones. And if I happen to find some, I'll add them to mine."

"That's…" Morgan didn't know what to say exactly. She took the penny passport from Adler, opened it, and saw the several open plastic slots for pressed pennies. "This is amazing, Addie."

"It's ridiculous. I just saw it and thought of you."

"Thank you," Morgan replied.

Adler stood. They stared at one another for a moment before Morgan placed the gift on the top bunk's bare mattress.

"How about we unpack the essentials and then go for a quick hike? There's a trail around here that's only a mile. We could do that, come back, and cook dinner," Morgan suggested.

"Sounds great."

"Tomorrow, I thought we could wake up early, take a kayak or canoe out on the water, and watch the sunrise."

"Really?" Adler asked. "That sounds perfect."

"I'll put all the food stuff in the container until we get back. Get ready, and I'll meet you outside," Morgan said.

She didn't wait for Adler to answer. She headed back out where she'd left the cooler and a couple of other things. She needed a moment to wrap her head around whatever was happening. She'd been trying to handle her growing feelings for Adler, knowing they'd never be returned. The vibe she'd been getting from the other woman, though, had her wondering if there was a chance there could be something between them after all. Now, she just needed to figure out what she was going to do about it.

CHAPTER 11

"YOU said that the hike would be easy," Adler said.

"No, I said it was short," Morgan replied with a laugh.

They dropped their packs onto the floor. Morgan flopped back onto the futon. Adler followed close behind. She looked over at Morgan. While the woman had sweat on her forehead and, likely, other places, she still looked great. Adler wondered how terrible *she* looked in comparison. The hike that she'd thought would be an easy mile had turned into a mostly uphill hike with a windy trail. She'd managed okay for most of it but realized fairly quickly that she was out of shape. She worked out as regularly as she could with her schedule, but running on a treadmill a few times a week hadn't prepared her for hiking at high elevation.

"Well, I'm definitely ready for dinner now," Adler replied. "How about I do the cooking tonight? You've done so much already."

"I thought we'd just do sandwiches or something tonight. We can keep it easy."

"Okay. I'll grab everything from the bear container and be right back."

Adler stood. Morgan didn't protest as Adler left the yurt. Just as she made it to the locked bear container to retrieve the food, her phone rang. Lake Tahoe had surprisingly good cell phone reception.

"Pax?"

"Hey. How are you?"

"I'm good. What's up?" Adler asked as she unlocked the container.

"How's Morgan?" Paxton asked.

"Gorgeous," Adler replied. "God, Pax. I like her. We just got back from a hike, and I stared at her ass for, like, half a mile. I just looked at the sweat on her forehead and thought about licking it off her skin."

"Wait... What?!" Paxton practically yelled and then laughed. "Seriously?"

"That's weird, right?" Adler asked, lifting the lid of the container. "Is this what it's like?"

"Is this *what* what's like?" Paxton asked.

"Being–"

"Gay?" Paxton interrupted. "You're asking me if wanting to lick another woman's sweat is a gay thing?"

"Pax, I don't know what's going on. I've only ever dated guys. I've only ever been interested in dating guys."

"But?"

"But since I first laid eyes on this woman, I've thought things I've never thought before."

"Sweat licking?"

"You're having way too much fun with this. What's the point of having a gay sister if I can't ask you these types of questions? Oh, and the sweat licking is a recent event."

"Adler, calm down. You're fine. Everything is fine."

"No, it's not, Pax."

"Why not?"

"Because I think she might be into me, too," Adler said softly, turning to make sure Morgan was still inside the yurt. "And I don't know what to do about it."

"What do you *want* to do about it?"

"I guess I want to talk to her."

"Talk? A minute ago, there was sweat licking. Now, you just want to talk?"

Adler turned back around to retrieve the food. When she did, she caught sight of something in between a few trees. It was large. It was black or brown. It had eyes. They were looking right at her.

"Pax, I have to go," she whispered.

"What? Is she there? Did she hear you? Please tell me

she heard you and you two are about to get it on inside a tiny tent. God, I can't believe my sister is into a woman. Mom and Dad are going to be so confused; two daughters in–"

"Bye, Pax," she whispered and hung up. "Morgan?" she said loudly enough for Morgan to, hopefully, hear. "Morgan, can you come out here, please?"

Adler stood completely still. The phone, while no longer connected to Paxton, was still in its position at her ear. Her other arm was at her side. Her feet were cement-stuck to the ground.

"What's up?" Morgan asked, moving toward her.

"No, stay there," Adler commanded. "Don't move."

"Addie, what's wrong?"

"There's something over there." She wanted to point, but she was afraid if she moved, she'd provoke it. "I'm pretty sure it's a bear."

"What?" Morgan walked up next to her and followed her line of sight. "Oh, that's a black bear." She shrugged.

"And it's about fifteen feet away from us," Adler said in a near-whisper.

"They're common here. We should close the container." Morgan reached down, closed and locked the container. Then, she yelled at the bear very, very loudly. A man came over from one of the other sites. He clanged a metal fork on a pan. Adler watched these two very crazy people as they continued to make noise. After a few seconds, the bear ran off and disappeared into the woods. "There. All good." Morgan turned to her. "Let's grab the food quickly, though. We can grab our shower stuff, too, but all soaps and everything needs to stay out here tonight. We can shower after dinner and lock it all back up."

"I'm sorry; there was a bear right over there." Adler pointed at the spot the bear used to occupy.

"Yeah, there was." Morgan laughed. "You're cute." She smiled at her. "Addie, this is the woods. We're in their territory, technically. With black bears, you just have to scare them off. Make yourself big. Make a lot of noise. That usually does the trick."

"And if that doesn't work, what? You run?"

"No, you never run," Morgan stated seriously.

"Morgan, we–"

"We're fine. That's Jake." She pointed to the man who had just helped her make as much noise as possible. "He works here. He does this all the time. He'll make sure the bear's run off. We're okay." She placed both of her soft hands on Adler's forearms. "I promise. I wouldn't take you out here if I didn't think we'd be safe."

"Okay." Adler nodded at those sincere blue eyes. "Dinner, then?"

"Go inside. I'll grab it."

"No way. I came out here to do something for you for once. Go back inside. If he comes back, I'll make a lot of noise."

Morgan chuckled and replied, "Just yell for me and for Jake."

"Go back inside," Adler said as she laughed.

Morgan disappeared back into their yurt. Just as she lifted the lid to the container again, her phone buzzed in her pocket. She thought it might be Paxton, making fun of her again, so she pulled it out. Instead of a text from her sister, she had a work email. For the first time in a long time, she had no desire to check it.

***

The coin-operated showers weren't exactly luxurious, but they were clean enough for Adler to feel comfortable. She took her time wiping her skin clean from the sweat and dirt of the day. She lathered and rinsed her hair, deciding she kind of liked the idea of letting it air-dry as she and Morgan sat by a fire Morgan had told her they'd build when they got done in the bathrooms. The only thing that made her uncomfortable about this whole trip so far, was the fact that

Morgan Burns was showering next to her. Morgan was in the adjacent stall. She was naked. Adler couldn't see her, of course, but she could sense her. She knew Morgan was doing exactly what she was doing to herself: her hands were roaming all over her body. Water and soap were mingling together to clean her skin. Her hair was being lathered and rinsed in the same way and, likely, with some fragrant shampoo. Adler sighed at the thought of walking into Morgan's shower stall. It was the most terrifying and exciting thought she'd ever had.

"Hey, I'm getting out. Are you about done?" Morgan's voice came from the next stall.

"Just finishing up." Adler pressed both hands to the wall in front of her and exhaled deeply. "Why don't you go out there? I'll catch up."

"What if you run into that mean bear?" Morgan asked, clearly mocking her.

"I think I can handle him now."

"You better hope it's a him; the females are worse, especially if they have their cubs nearby."

"Wait... What? Cubs?"

Morgan's laughter rang out through the small building until Adler was all alone in the shower room. She ran both hands up and down her face rapidly, trying to come to grips with whatever it was she was feeling. Then, she slid one hand down between her legs and tentatively stroked. The immediate surge of electricity confirmed what she already knew. The surprising wetness and hardness only added to the confirmation. Adler Williams wanted Morgan Burns.

She finished up her shower, dressed, and made her way back toward the campsite. Morgan was sitting at the picnic table, shuffling a deck of cards. She smiled as Adler approached. The fire Morgan had already built wasn't roaring, but it was going, providing Adler the complete camping experience. Adler sat down across from her.

"War?" she asked.

"Let's do it," Morgan said.

After several hands, Adler slid the cards back into their pack. She stood, made her way over to the fire, and sat on one of the three small logs surrounding it. Morgan joined her moments later. They didn't speak for a long time. Every so often, Adler would toss a small stick onto the dying fire. Eventually, Morgan stood and put out the fire. Adler helped her pack everything in the bear container. They made their way inside the yurt, where Morgan took off her shoes. She sat on the futon for a moment. Again, neither of them said anything. Adler slid off her boots and sat down next to her.

"Top or bottom? Or do you want the futon?" Adler asked. "I'm okay anywhere."

"I guess I can take the top bunk if you're taking the bottom. If you're taking the futon, then I'll just take the bottom."

"I don't care. You can decide," Adler said.

"I don't care, either," Morgan replied.

"This is ridiculous." Adler laughed.

"I'll flip you a pressed penny for the futon?" Morgan asked.

"Deal." Adler stood and moved to the package she'd yet to stow. She removed one of the pennies, looked at Morgan, and said, "Call it."

"I'll take the shiny back over the design side," she replied.

Adler flipped the coin into the air, caught it in her hand, pressed to the backside of the other one, and lifted the hand.

"You're on the futon," she said.

"A deal's a deal," Morgan replied.

"We could always share it," Adler suggested with a hard swallow.

"Yes," Morgan whispered. "We could."

CHAPTER 12

THEY laid out their sleeping bags on top of the now flat futon. Morgan was careful with her words and with her motions. The idea to share the futon had been Adler's, but Morgan didn't want to make any comments that might scare her away from wanting to do it. Morgan slid into her own sleeping bag and zipped it as if she were sleeping alone. That way Adler wouldn't think she was planning on trying anything. Adler had been giving her hints. That was true. But hints didn't necessarily mean Adler was interested in pursuing something with her.

"Warm?" Adler turned onto her side to face her. "The space heater is on, and you're all bundled up. Everything okay?"

"Yeah, I'm good." Morgan turned to face her.

"What if I'm cold?"

"That's my spare sleeping bag. It'll keep you warm even if it's freezing outside. And it's not–" Adler slid closer to her. "Oh, you weren't referring to the–"

"No, I wasn't." Adler rested her head on her elbow.

"Addie, what's going on?" Morgan mimicked Adler's posture. "You know what you're doing, right? That you're saying and doing things that are kind of confusing me."

"I know," Adler replied. "I can't help it."

"Can't help torturing me?" Morgan asked and rolled onto her back.

"I'm torturing you?" Adler slid just a little bit closer to her. "I don't mean to torture you, Morgan."

"What do you mean to do?"

"Figure out what I'm feeling," Adler replied. "I've never–"

"I get it," Morgan interrupted. "You have a confusing feeling that you need to work out, but you're straight. You like me, but you don't think you'd ever be able to do anything about–"

"Hey! Maybe let me be the one to tell you how I'm feeling instead of you thinking you know, huh?" she asked and smiled.

"It's okay, Addie. I get it. I've heard it before."

"Heard what before?" Adler asked.

"It happens, sometimes, with straight women. They–"

"I'm not experimenting, Morgan," Adler interrupted.

"No, that's not what I'm saying," Morgan replied, turning to face her. "Let's just drop this subject." She laughed more out of nervousness than anything else. "Our friendship is important to me, Addie. I don't want to mess it up."

"No one's doing that, Morgan." Adler met Morgan's eyes with her own soft gray ones. Her hand moved to Morgan's cheek. She rested it there, not moving her fingers or thumb to caress. "I don't know what's happening."

"Addie, if you don't know that, then I don't think anything should happen," Morgan suggested. "I don't know what you're feeling. I don't want to call it an experiment, because I know that's not you. I believe you when you say that. I just don't think anything should happen *now*." She paused. "At least not until you – I don't know – figure out if you want something more than friendship."

"I think I already know that," Adler said.

"You *think*? Addie, even if you do know you *want* more… Do you know if you *can* do more, have more with me?" Morgan asked.

Adler's hand moved from her cheek. Morgan knew then that Adler wasn't ready. The expression in her eyes said that even more than the fact that they were no longer touching. Morgan tried not to give any indication that she was disappointed. She didn't want Adler to feel sorry for her or do something she wasn't ready to do because Morgan wanted something more between them. Just lying next to Adler like this had Morgan's skin on fire. She licked her lips unconsciously, thinking of what Adler's lips would feel like pressed against any and every part of her body.

"It's been a long day," Adler said and rolled onto her back. "Let's get some sleep. We can talk about this tomorrow."

Morgan unzipped her sleeping bag and replied, "Okay." She stood and lifted the sleeping bag to hold in front of her. "I'm going to sleep on the bottom bunk, okay?"

"Morgan, you don't–"

"It's not because of you, Addie. It's for me." Morgan gave Adler a look that she hoped expressed that this wasn't the woman's fault. Then, she turned, placed her sleeping bag flat on the mattress, slid inside and zipped it up. "Night, Addie."

***

When Adler woke up, Morgan wasn't in bed. She stretched, removed herself from the sleeping bag and stood. She changed into what she'd assumed she'd need to wear on the water. Morgan walked into the yurt just as she slid on her shoes.

"Good morning," Morgan said.

"Hey," Adler replied not knowing what else to say. "Are we still going to watch the sunrise over the water, or did I sleep too late?"

"The sun's up, I'm afraid." Morgan gave her an apologetic look. "But I didn't want to wake you up. You looked like you were out like a light and maybe needed the sleep."

"I'm sorry. It took me forever to fall asleep. I think it was around one when I finally did."

"It's okay. We can do it tomorrow before we leave." Morgan walked past her to retrieve something from her pack.

"What do you want to do today?" Adler asked, sitting on the edge of the still pulled out futon.

"I thought we'd maybe go to the beach."

"Perfect. I'm wearing my suit under here. I'm ready when you are."

"I was outside, packing something to eat for lunch. Just let me get changed, and I'll meet you out there."

A few minutes later, they drove the short distance from the campsite to the beach. They said nothing as Morgan drove them. Adler knew something had changed between them. Their banter and usual way with one another had disappeared. When they laid out a blanket and sat down next to one another, it was with enough space between them that clearly indicated Morgan didn't want to be close. Adler didn't bother asking if Morgan would help her apply sunscreen. She'd, apparently, been torturing Morgan this whole time. She didn't want to add to it and make Morgan feel bad. They sat next to one another for a while, making occasional small talk. The beach had a few people on it, but not all that many. The weather was warm without being overly hot. The water was clear and beautiful. Then, Adler turned to see Morgan was standing up. The woman removed her shirt, revealing a navy-blue bikini top. Adler's eyes went wide.

"I'm going to cool off," Morgan said, sliding her cargo shorts down her legs and revealing matching bottoms.

"Okay," Adler replied.

As Morgan walked to the water, Adler stared at her. Morgan stood at the water's edge for a moment, testing the temperature with her feet. Once she seemed comfortable, she took a few steps into it. A few minutes later, she was waist deep and tossing water over her face and hair. She turned to look over her shoulder at Adler then.

Adler Williams had never been more turned on in her life. Morgan's smile lit up the world. Her eyes somehow managed to reflect the water and look even brighter than before. Adler swallowed hard. Morgan turned around to face the lake. Adler stood and removed her own clothing. She stalled a little by stacking everything into a neat pile for when they returned. Then, she headed out into the water.

"I want to hold you," she whispered into Morgan's ear from behind. "It's all I can think about. You're so beautiful, Morgan."

"Addie, you—"

Adler's arms wrapped around Morgan's waist, locking themselves together on her abdomen. Morgan's body was stiff for several moments before it finally relaxed into Adler's embrace.

"I've never wanted to hold another woman like this before," Adler said softly.

"How does it feel?"

"Really, really good," she answered. "Things have been weird between us since last night, Morgan. I don't want that."

"What do you want?"

"I think I'd like to kiss you."

"You think?" Morgan asked, covering Adler's hands with her own.

"No, I *know*." Adler shook her head. "I know that's what I want. I'm just scared, Morgan."

Morgan turned in her arms. Suddenly, they were closer than they'd ever been. Morgan's eyes were boring into her own. Morgan's lips were inches away. Adler knew she could taste them if she wanted to. All she had to do was lean in.

"Of me?" Morgan asked, bringing Adler's attention back to her eyes. "Are you scared of me?"

"What? No." Adler's arms went around the other woman's waist again. Morgan's stayed at her side. "I'm scared because I don't know what to do. I understand the mechanics, obviously. But, Morgan, I grew up with a sister who came out to me. I've met a lot of lesbians. And I've never once thought about doing what we're doing right now."

"We're not really doing anything yet," Morgan reminded.

"Yes, we are." Adler pulled her in closer. "It started the day we met. It's been going this whole time. And last night, Morgan, we finally acknowledged it."

"Adler, I have had a few relationships go badly. One

of them was with the person I thought I'd spend the rest of my life with."

"Reese," Adler said, remembering how Morgan talked to her for hours about what had happened between them. She recalled Morgan's pain, but she also recalled her own. She'd been sad for herself because she'd never had a Reese. Brad had been the closest thing she'd found to love. And looking back, she wasn't even sure that was what it was between the two of them. She'd also been upset because Reese had a piece of Morgan that Adler never could. "Morgan, I don't know what's going to happen between us, but I don't want to hurt you. You know that, right?"

"Addie, if you're scared because you've never done this before, I'm scared because I have. I've fallen for a best friend. It didn't work. You've been my best friend since we met. Kinsley has Riley now. Reese has Kellan. Remy has Ryan. Everyone I know has found their someone except me. And if you and I–"

Adler leaned in before the woman could finish. She pressed her lips fleetingly to Morgan's. It was a peck. It was chaste. It could just have easily been a light kiss exchanged between two friends. But it was enough to shut Morgan up for a second. A second was all Adler needed.

"Did you ever stop to think that it ended between you and Reese and those other women because they weren't *the* someone for you, and you needed to wait until *your* someone showed up?"

"Yes, but–"

"Morgan, I'm standing in front of you, in this beautiful lake, holding you because I want to kiss you. I want you to kiss me back. I don't know anything else right now, but I do know that."

Morgan pulled away from her arms and replied, "I don't think that's enough, Addie." She shrugged. "I don't think I can risk my heart again with someone who only knows she wants to kiss me but doesn't know anything beyond that." She looked at the beach. "What happens after we kiss? What if you don't like it? What if you do, and we try this, but it ends? I don't think I can lose you as a friend." Morgan slid her hand into Adler's, squeezed it, and then let it go. "Let's just take some time to try to get things back to normal."

"Normal?"

"Just friends, Addie. Let's get back to that."

Morgan walked through the water and onto the beach. Adler stared out across the water for a moment before she turned, walked back to the beach, and grabbed Morgan's arm. She turned the woman around, pulled her into her body, and kissed her.

CHAPTER 13

GOD, Adler could kiss. Morgan had taken several steps backward with the force of Adler's mouth on her own. Once she regained her balance, her arms wrapped around Adler's neck. She pulled Adler even closer, allowing their tongues to join the kiss. Her fingers played at the back of Adler's neck. Adler's hands were on her hips but remained still. Morgan could feel Adler's thumbs pressing firmly into her hip bones. She wanted to tell her it was okay to move, to touch, but she didn't want to end their first real kiss. Adler's lips were soft. Her skin was just as soft, if not softer. It was also wet from their swim. Well, they hadn't actually done any swimming. Her skin was wet all the same. Morgan ran her fingers around to Adler's throat. She lowered them over her chest, not stopping to cup her breasts, but graze them. As she passed over them with the fleeting touch, Adler moaned. Morgan felt it in her depths.

Adler's hands finally moved around Morgan's waist. She rubbed up and down Morgan's back as their kiss continued. Morgan's legs suddenly didn't feel all that strong. She backed them up until she could feel their blanket under her foot. Reluctantly, she pulled their eager mouths apart. Adler's eyes opened, immediately concerned. Morgan smiled at their darkened hue. Then, she looked around. There were two other groups of beachgoers on this less popular tourist attraction. One group was in the water, about fifty yards away, and not paying any attention to them. Another couple was lying on their own blanket, but again, focused on themselves and the water. Morgan tugged on Adler's hands, moving to her knees. Then, she pulled Adler down to lie next to her. She stared down at Adler, running her hand over her bare stomach, grateful for the bikini the woman was wearing.

"We've kissed," Morgan said. "We're in the next part now, Addie. This is the part where you tell me what happens now, because I really want to kiss you again. I want to touch you."

"Then, kiss me, Morgan." Adler reached to cup her cheek.

Morgan leaned down. This time, she initiated the contact. She pressed their lips together once, twice, and then a third time, placed her hand flat over Adler's stomach and connected them again. She pulled Adler's bottom lip into her mouth. She sucked on it softly. Adler let out a tiny whimper, which Morgan guessed was a good thing. She slid the tip of her tongue over the lip before she slid it inside Adler's mouth. Adler's hand went to the back of Morgan's neck, pulling her in closer. Before Morgan knew it, she was on top of Adler. She knew there were people around, but she didn't care. She couldn't care. She'd had fantasies about kissing this woman. She was finally living them. Her hands flattened against the blanket on either side of Adler's head. Adler's tongue mingled with her own for several moments while her hands seemed to be fidgeting at Morgan's back. Morgan could feel Adler's fingers playing with the string holding her bikini top on. Morgan pulled back only for a moment before she pressed her lips to Adler's neck.

"Be careful there. You might end up taking my top off in public," Morgan said and chuckled against Adler's heated skin.

"Shit. Sorry." Adler's hands stilled.

"Don't be sorry." Morgan sucked Adler's earlobe into her mouth. "Do you want to take my top off?"

"Not on a public beach," Adler replied.

Morgan laughed softly into Adler's ear and said, "But you do want to take it off?"

"Yes," Adler whispered.

Morgan smiled through the kiss she applied to Adler's

chest just above her left breast. She kissed the same spot over her right one before looking up and meeting Adler's eyes. She slid some unruly hair from Adler's face with one hand as her other placed feather-light touches to Adler's stomach.

"This is nice," Morgan said. "Just being able to touch you like this."

"Yes, it is." Adler lifted herself up on her elbows. "But I'd kind of like to return to the kissing if we can." She gave Morgan an expression that told the woman she was definitely serious.

"You don't think we should slow down and, maybe, talk?"

"Talk later," Adler replied, reaching for the back of Morgan's neck. "I've been thinking about kissing you since that night in Jackson Hole."

Morgan was pulled down to Adler's lips. She wasn't complaining. Those lips felt like her home. They were pliant against her own, without being too giving or too demanding. The kiss ebbed and flowed naturally for several minutes, with Morgan's lips moving away every so often to taste Adler's skin. When her tongue licked up the side of Adler's neck, Morgan felt Adler's legs open slightly. On instinct, she slipped a thigh between them. Adler gasped but didn't stop the kiss, begging for more by jutting her tongue deep into Morgan's mouth. Morgan rocked into her once and then again, testing the waters. Adler gave her back soft sounds. Her hands moved to Morgan's lower back and stilled.

Morgan moved her mouth again to the neck she was already growing to love kissing. As she did, she opened her eyes to her right to see the couple, that had been there moments before, had left. She looked sideways into the water to see the three people, that had been standing out there moments before, had climbed into a canoe. She could see them on the water, rowing away from the beach. Morgan's mouth moved lower then. She kissed those spots above

Adler's breasts. Her thigh pressed into Adler again. When Adler didn't resist, she rocked into her slowly while her lips lowered still. She kissed the bikini top over the spot where Adler's nipple would be. She felt it harden beneath her lips. Adler let out a soft, almost imperceptible gasp. Morgan sucked the nipple through the top.

"Is this okay?" she asked.

"Yes, but is anyone–"

"Everyone's gone," Morgan interrupted and rolled into her again. "It's just us here."

"Are you sure?" Adler asked.

Morgan lifted herself up and looked to both sides. Adler lifted up her own head to check the water. Morgan glanced off at the distant parking lot, seeing no cars save her own. Then, she was promptly pulled back down to Adler's mouth. Her thigh continued to work between Adler's legs. Her mouth moved away from Adler's greedy one, back to the woman's breasts. She sucked on the other nipple in the same way, feeling the wetness pool between her thighs. Her clit had already turned rock-hard and swollen from her ministrations against Adler's covered sex.

"Addie, we–"

"If you keep doing what you're doing, you'll make me come, Morgan," Adler said softly.

Morgan stopped moving immediately, not knowing what to do.

"Morgan, make me come," Adler added just as softly. "Like this. Just like this." She lifted her hips up and into Morgan's thigh. "This feels really good."

"God, Adler." Morgan rocked slowly again, lowering herself onto Adler's thigh. "Is this okay?"

"Are you–" Adler started and stopped. "I mean, are you–"

"Turned on as hell? Yes." Morgan kissed her hard. "Are you sure you want to do this here?"

"I don't think I can move until you make me come," Adler answered. "I'm so–"

Morgan captured her lips. She kissed Adler hard, rocking her center against Adler's thigh, feeling her own orgasm build as she pressed her hand over Adler's bikini bottoms. She left it there as she rocked her own thigh rhythmically against Adler's sex.

"Addie, this is–"

"I want it, Morgan." Adler grunted as she gripped Morgan's ass, pressing the woman further into herself. "I want you. God, I want you."

Morgan's eyes closed with those remarkable words. Then, she opened them to look down at the woman beneath her. Adler's chest was heaving. Her breasts were rising and falling as Morgan continued to cup her. Morgan allowed one finger to press slightly harder between Adler's legs. Adler bucked up to meet it. Morgan felt the wetness against her own skin and her suit bottoms. She knew she'd likely leave some behind on Adler's bare thigh.

"Addie, I'm going–"

"Yes." Adler held on to Morgan's ass more tightly. Morgan stared down at her and watched as it happened. "Yes, Morgan. Harder. I'm–"

Adler came against her hand; her hips were lifting up and down, taking her pleasure. The sight alone was enough to make Morgan climax.

"Addie, I'm coming. I'm coming."

"I can feel it," Adler said. Morgan wasn't sure what she was referring to for a moment, until Adler added, "I can feel you on my leg. Wow."

"Yes. Yes." Morgan's hips rocked hard, pressing her down further into Adler's thigh.

When she finally came down, she was still on top of Adler. Their whole bodies pressed together, with Adler running her fingers up and down Morgan's damp back.

"I think the people on that canoe are coming back this way," Adler said after a few minutes. "We should probably move." Adler patted her on the back as if to ask Morgan to get off her.

Morgan lifted herself up and asked, "Addie, are you–"

Adler laughed and said, "Morgan, I'm fine. *We* are fine. I just think we should get off this beach." She paused. "And no offense to that yurt, but I'd really like to spend tonight in your house. There's a very nice bedroom there."

"With a very nice bed," Morgan added.

"Yes, that's the idea."

Morgan moved to lie beside the woman. She ran her hand over Adler's still flushed skin.

"Addie?"

"Yeah?" Adler turned on her side to face her.

"How do you feel right now?" Morgan pecked her lips once, just in case whatever followed from Addie's lips meant she'd never get to do it again.

"I feel like I need to process what we just did," she said.

Morgan gulped.

"Not like that," Adler added, cupping Morgan's cheek and reading her expression. "I kissed you, Morgan."

"You did."

"And then you kissed me."

"Yes."

"And then I told you to make me come on a beach where we weren't technically alone," Adler said with a laugh. "I can't believe I did that."

"Do you regret it?"

Adler shook her head and said, "Not even a little bit." She paused as she ran her thumb over Morgan's slightly swollen lips. "But tonight, I don't know if we should–"

"Go further?" Morgan guessed.

"I did not plan on what just happened." She laughed and looked at the sky. "I was just in the moment and knew what I wanted."

"But now that your brain is doing the thinking, you'd like to take things a little slower," Morgan replied.

"Not too slow," Adler said with a wink in her direction. "I leave in less than two weeks. I plan to make use of my time in South Lake Tahoe." She smiled at Morgan, running her thumb over the woman's top lip this time. "Let's, maybe, get out of here and hit the showers?"

Morgan nodded. As they packed, they hardly touched. Morgan knew it was her doing. She hadn't exactly planned this, either. It was amazing. She wanted more soon, but it was also very fast. Adler hadn't ever done anything with a woman. That added a layer of complications. But the main reason Morgan was now not entirely happy was that the woman she'd just had sex with on the beach and wanted to spend as much time with as possible, was leaving for Seattle in less than two weeks.

CHAPTER 14

HAD she just had sex on the beach? Had she just had sex on a beach with a woman? They'd both had an orgasm. Of that, she was certain. She hadn't touched Morgan. Morgan hadn't really touched her. God, Morgan hadn't even really touched her. Adler had come so hard, she worried her cries would be heard by the people on the canoe. She'd never had sex in public. That wasn't true anymore. She'd come at Morgan's touch, with Morgan's eyes boring into her own at one point. Adler hadn't turned away. Morgan hadn't turned away. It had been a perfect first time, and she wasn't even sure if it counted as a first time.

"Pax?"

"Hey. What's up?" Paxton asked a few hours later, when Adler called her from just beyond the tree line while Morgan was inside the yurt, packing their things.

"I have a question. It's going to sound ignorant and dumb, and I'm sorry in advance. I don't mean to offend you or any other lesbians. I–"

"Adler, I think you've given me enough of the PC stuff. What's going on?" Paxton laughed.

Adler turned back to the yurt, to ensure Morgan was still inside, and she asked, "What counts as lesbian sex?"

After Paxton's loud laughter finally died down enough for the woman to answer her, she replied, "Why do you need to know?"

"Because I think I might have just had sex with Morgan," Adler replied, squinting her eyes for no reason.

"I'm sorry... Did you just say you had sex with a woman?"

"I don't *know* if I had sex with a woman; that's what I'm saying," Adler returned.

"How do you *not* know if you had sex with a woman, Adler?" Paxton fired back.

"Because I've never done it before. Don't give me a hard time about this. When you were twelve, you asked me if French kissing could only be done in France."

"I was twelve, Adler. You're an adult. You know how it all works."

"Pax, I need my sister right now. Please."

"Okay. Okay. Tell me what you two did."

"We were on the beach," Adler said.

"Hold on… You had sex on a beach in Lake Tahoe? Like, a public beach, where people were around?"

"Paxton, let me get through this."

"Okay. Sorry," Paxton replied.

"We were in the water. Actually, I followed her out to the water." Adler closed her eyes to recall how it felt to hold Morgan from behind. "I wrapped my arms around her, Pax. I just held her, and it was perfect. She said some things. I said some things. I gave her this peck on her lips. She said we should just be friends, but I didn't want that. I followed her back to the beach, and I kissed her."

"You kissed her? Twice?"

"More than twice, but that part's later," she answered. "We had a blanket. We were lying there, making out. And, I guess, the few people that had been there were either gone or far enough away, because, one minute – we were just kissing, and the next – she was on top of me, with her leg between mine, and–"

"Damn, Adler. Who started tearing off the clothes first?"

"We didn't do that," Adler replied. "We were in our bathing suits; we didn't take anything off. She didn't actually touch me." Adler blushed. "This might be too much information, but she kind of just held me there, over my bottoms, and moved against me."

"And did you…"

"Yes," Adler answered her sister's obvious question.

"Did she?"

"Yes."

"Do you know for sure?"

"Why? Do you think she'd fake it?"

"No, Adler. I guess I'm just trying to see where your confusion is here. You two both had orgasms while touching the other person. I mean, did you get naked? No. Did she technically touch your skin? No. None of that matters, though."

"Because we both had orgasms?" Adler asked.

"You're so dumb sometimes."

"Paxton…"

"Adler, how did it feel when you were with her? When she touched you wherever and however she touched you? When she came because of you and you did because of her?"

"Amazing," Adler replied. "It was amazing."

"Then, Adler Williams, I am beyond thrilled to tell you that in your younger sister's very lesbian opinion, you just had sex with a woman." She sighed. "Adler, I don't think that's right, actually."

"Wait… What?" Adler turned again to check that Morgan was still inside the yurt. When she turned, though, she caught Morgan's eye as the woman spotted her and started her way with the brightest eyes and the biggest smile Adler had ever seen. "Beautiful," she whispered.

"Oh, Adler. You didn't just have sex with Morgan. You two made love," Paxton replied.

***

"Everything okay?" Morgan asked when she approached.

"I was just talking to my sister," Adler replied, stuffing the phone into her pocket.

Morgan stood a few feet away from her. She hadn't tried to take her hand earlier when they'd driven back to the site or even when they'd walked to the yurt. She hadn't tried to kiss her again, either. Adler wondered if she was giving off signals that said she didn't want to be touched. Then, she recalled her statement on the beach about needing time to process.

"I packed everything into the car. We're good to go whenever you're ready," Morgan said.

"Can we go on a walk before we go? There's this spot we passed on our hike yesterday. I'd like to see it again if that's okay," she replied.

"Let's go, then," Morgan said with a smile. "You lead the way."

They hadn't hiked more than about ten minutes before Adler stopped them. She moved away from the trail and into the large grouping of massive pine trees. The wind, lightly cascading over their needles, provided that rustling sound and woodsy scent she'd wanted when she'd thought about taking Morgan here. Morgan followed her and stood in front of her as Adler looked up at the trees. She lowered her eyes to Morgan's, moved into her, and stroked the woman's cheek.

"I know what I said earlier about needing time to think about things," she began. "And I know that's unfair to you, Morgan."

"Addie, it's–"

"Morgan, I think the scary part for me isn't that I don't know how I feel. It's that I *do* know how I feel." She moved closer to Morgan. "This place is beautiful. Seeing the mountains with you that night, watching the sunset with you, that was beautiful. What you said, about being out there with the right person, was correct, Morgan. I knew it then. I said as much."

"And I'm that person?" Morgan asked her.

"Yes, I think you are." Adler smiled at her. "And I'd like to go back to your place, cook you dinner, and I want to hold you again. I don't want you to shy away from touching me because this is all new to me. I don't want you to think I don't want this. I *do* want this. I want to hold your hand, meet your friends while I'm here, and try to figure out with you how this could work with me in Seattle and you here. I want to kiss you. I'd like you to kiss me how you did on that beach." She leaned in and pressed her lips to Morgan's as she'd done in the water. "And I'd like us to do other things, too."

"Tonight, how about we do that dinner?" Morgan kissed her lips just as gently. "And talk?"

"How is it possible that I went on a vacation with my boyfriend and met my best friend that was always supposed to be something more?" Adler asked.

"Life's crazy that way, I guess," Morgan said. "I'm going to kiss you how I kissed you on the beach now."

Adler smiled as Morgan leaned in and took her lips. She kissed her hard and slow. Then, deep and fast. Adler's hands moved to Morgan's waist. She slid them under Morgan's T-shirt and felt only skin.

"You're not wearing a bra," Adler said, pulling away from the kiss.

"Nope," Morgan replied with a smirk. "I thought we were driving home. *You* decided to take us on a little hike."

"Jesus, Morgan." Adler's hands moved to Morgan's abdomen where they rested just below the woman's breasts. "I want to—"

"Do it," Morgan encouraged.

"If I do, I won't want to stop. If what happened on the beach is any indication, I can't just touch you without wanting more."

"Keep it in your pants there, Williams. We've managed to avoid one arrest today for lewd behavior. I don't think we should take any chances." Morgan pulled Adler's hands out from under her shirt and kissed each palm in turn. "Come on. Let's go home."

Adler took Morgan's hand. They walked out of the trees and back to the trail hand in hand. When a couple past them headed in the other direction, Adler noticed the man holding the woman's hand. They were smiling at one another. She looked over to Morgan and smiled at her. They made their way to the trailhead and into the car. Morgan reached immediately for her hand after putting the key in the ignition and starting it up. She moved Adler's hand to her own lap, holding on to it as she backed them out of the parking lot. A few minutes after they'd gotten on the main road back to Morgan's house, Morgan used both hands to turn left. Adler seized the moment and ran her hand up and down Morgan's thigh, noting how hard it was beneath her touch.

"God, you're in shape," Adler said mainly to herself. "Your body is flat in the right places and muscled in the right places."

"Is that a compliment?" Morgan asked as she made the turn.

"Yes, that's definitely a compliment. Morgan, you're hot." She squeezed Morgan's thigh before sliding her own hand up higher, leaving it in place when she heard a gasp. "Problem?" Adler asked.

"I thought I told you to keep it in your pants," Morgan said.

"You could always pull it away," Adler suggested, leaning over a little closer.

"God, why would I do that?" Morgan chuckled. Adler's fingertips danced over the fabric of Morgan's cargo shorts at the apex of her thighs. "Addie!"

"How does it feel?" Adler asked.

"Like I might drive us off the road. What happened to cooking dinner and talking?"

Adler moved two fingertips up and down. She watched Morgan's eyes close for only a second before opening again. She couldn't believe she was having this kind of effect on this woman just by lightly grazing her through her shorts.

"I don't know. I know that's the right thing to do; we should talk. I just also know I like watching you like this. I liked it earlier, too."

"Earlier?" Morgan asked through a gasp.

"When you were on top of me."

"Fuck." Morgan stopped at the red light. She looked

over at Adler. "You can't talk about that while you're doing what you're doing to me."

Adler applied more pressure with her fingers and asked, "Could you come like this?"

"Yes," Morgan whispered. "I've been on edge all day. Hell, I've been on edge since last night. I'm driving, though, Addie."

"Then, drive. I'll do all the work."

"I swear to God, I am going to get you back for this." Morgan chuckled again but stopped as Adler pressed into her harder.

"I hope so," Adler said.

She moved her fingers up and down several more times. Morgan hit the gas a little harder than she likely intended when the light changed. Adler used it as her opportunity to unbutton the shorts and lower the zipper.

"Oh, fuck," Morgan said and swallowed hard.

Adler watched Morgan's face as she slid her hand down over her underwear.

"It's only fair; you touched me like this on the beach." She cupped Morgan and pressed hard. "I can feel you."

"You made me wet," Morgan said with her eyes still on the road.

Adler leaned over further still. She pressed two fingers through Morgan's underwear and into her clit.

"Oh, God," Adler muttered. "You feel…"

"Just don't stop. You started it. Don't stop," Morgan said as she slowed for another red light. "Make me come, Addie."

Adler stroked Morgan through the thin fabric of her underwear, wondering what color they were. She couldn't see much from her position and with Morgan's T-shirt covering up part of what she was doing. She didn't want to move anything right now other than her fingers against Morgan's body. She was touching a woman while that woman was driving them back to her house. Her hand would come away from that woman's body coated with her arousal. Morgan's hips tried to buck but couldn't. Adler smirked at the fact that she was doing this to her. When the light turned to green, Morgan pressed the gas pedal. That small movement must have done something to her because she came in Adler's hand then. She called out Adler's name, pressed her own palm against Adler's, and closed her eyes for a few seconds before opening them again.

"That's the sexiest thing I've ever seen," Adler said when Morgan came down.

"That's the sexiest thing I've ever done," Morgan replied with flushed cheeks.

CHAPTER 15

"DINNER was amazing. Thank you," Morgan said, kissing Adler's neck from behind.

"You're welcome. Now, go relax in the living room or something."

Adler was rinsing the dishes from their shared meal. She hadn't allowed Morgan to help cook, set the table or anything. Now, she wasn't even letting her do the dishes.

"I could just go upstairs," Morgan said as she wrapped her arms around Adler's waist. "And get ready for bed."

"Did you overexert yourself today?" Adler asked.

Morgan could feel Adler's smirk. She kissed her neck again and slid her arms under Adler's shirt, pressing her hands flat to the woman's stomach.

"I definitely didn't overexert myself." She flicked Adler's earlobe back and forth with her tongue. "I think you'll discover that men overexert themselves while women usually have no problem going all night long."

"Morgan…" Adler whispered.

Morgan's hands slid a little lower to rest on the waistband of Adler's jeans as she said, "Yes?"

"Go into the living room and relax." Adler used her butt to give Morgan a slight shove backward. She laughed when Morgan grunted a little. "I'll be right in. I'll bring wine."

Morgan smiled at Adler, kissed her on the shoulder, and moved, as ordered, into the living room. She decided to start a fire in her wood-burning, newly refurbished fireplace. The dark and light color bricks mingled together to provide just the right combination of colors for just about any occasion. Morgan placed several logs inside, and deciding she didn't want to waste time, she tossed in the starter log, lit it, used the poker to get everything in the right place to produce a romantic, roaring fire, and looked on for a moment.

"Nice fire," Adler said when she entered the room. She passed Morgan a glass of red wine and held one to her own lips. "Romantic."

"That was the idea," Morgan said, turning to her. They clinked glasses, took a sip, and sat on the sofa next to one another. "Movie?"

"Dinner and a movie? Perfect first date." Adler smiled at her. "We just had dessert, but do you have popcorn? I could make some."

"I do. James eats it by the bucketful when she's here."

"I'll make some," Adler said, moving to stand.

"Addie, sit." Morgan pulled her back to the sofa. "You're all anxious now, aren't you?"

"It's just that we're actually in private for the first time since–"

"We came together on a beach?" Morgan finished for her with a smile.

"Yes," Adler said.

"Addie, nothing's going to happen tonight if you don't want it to. We really can just have dinner and a movie, with or without the popcorn. I'd like it if you slept in my bed tonight instead of the guest room, but we don't have to do anything." She placed her hand on Adler's thigh. "Although, I do think it's interesting how in the car earlier, you had no problem touching. Now, you're all adorably nervous."

"I'm not nervous," Adler argued.

"Liar," Morgan said with a laugh. "And Addie?"

"Yeah?"

"So am I."

"But you've done this before. And today, we…"

"Adler, it's true that I've been with other women, but that doesn't have any bearing on what happens with us. It doesn't work that way. I'm not comparing you to anyone. Today was the best day, Addie. When we met in Wyoming,

I thought I had a crush. When I got back here, I told James and my other friends all about you. They all worried that I'd fallen for some straight girl. Truthfully, I worried about that, too. It's why I've tried to be careful with you. I didn't want to get my heart broken." She squeezed Adler's thigh. "I know I still might. That's true in any relationship; one or both of us might want to get out of this one day. But, right now, I want to be with you. I'm not thinking about how anyone I've been with is the same or different than you. All I can think about is you."

"Hey, Morgan?"

"Huh?" Morgan moved to reach for her wine.

"Take me upstairs."

Morgan stopped in her tracks. She moved to lean back against the sofa, looking at Adler's beautiful face.

"We're not good at stopping once we start, Addie. Are you sure?"

"Oh, my God." Adler stood. "Is this what it means to date a woman? Are you going to ask me a hundred times if I'm sure before you tear my clothes off?" She laughed.

Morgan stood up next to her and asked, "Would you rather I not ask anymore and just took what I want?"

"Yes." Adler swallowed so hard, Morgan could see every movement in her throat.

Morgan reached for the button on Adler's jeans. She unbuttoned them and pulled down on the zipper. She caught Adler's eyes watching her. Neither of them said anything. Adler's eyes were a dark gray now. Her tongue slid out to lick her lips. Morgan's did the same in response. She moved into Adler's space, reaching around her lower back to pull down on the jeans. Adler moved back a step in an attempt to remain balanced. Morgan pushed the woman back even further, until she had Adler on the wall next to the fireplace. When Adler said nothing, she kneeled down in front of her, kissing Adler at the top of her underwear. Adler made one of those whimpers Morgan already liked so much. Morgan moved to stand again. She stared into Adler's eyes and slid her own hand into the woman's jeans. This time, she didn't stop above the underwear. She went below it.

"Oh," Adler muttered.

"This is what I want. You said to take it." Morgan leaned into Adler.

She kissed Adler's neck as her fingers moved into slick folds. Morgan stroked slowly, enjoying the feel of Adler's wetness against her fingers. She sucked on Adler's earlobe. When she did, the woman's hips bucked into her hand.

"I want more, Morgan," Adler said as her arms wrapped around Morgan's neck.

"Remember what I said about how women can go all night long?" She flicked at Adler's earlobe with the tip of her tongue. "This is only the beginning."

She squeezed Adler's clit between two fingers. Adler gripped her behind the neck in response. Morgan slid her thigh between Adler's, pressing it into the hand that was working between them. She rocked her own center over Adler's thigh as she applied more focused attention to Adler's clit.

"I'll come," Adler said on a breath. "If you don't stop or slow down, I'll come."

"Good," Morgan replied, using two fingers to flick Adler's clit back and forth, up and down, and then in slow circles.

"Morgan, I'm coming," Adler said.

Her hands were in Morgan's hair. She tugged and pulled until Morgan's face was in front of her own. Then, she kissed Morgan hard. Her own moans were quieted by Morgan's mouth as she came. The moment Adler's tremors subsided, Morgan slid her fingers out. She gripped Adler's shirt and yanked it off, revealing a lilac-colored bra beneath. Morgan pulled her own shirt off, tossing it to the floor to join Adler's. She unclasped her own bra, dropping it onto the gathering pile. Adler's eyes went immediately to her breasts. Her hands moved to cup them. Morgan groaned at the contact. Her breasts were already swollen with need. Her nipples were already erect and hard. By the time Adler touched them, it was painful, but in that way that the pain of their hardness was balanced with the pleasure.

"I want your bra off," Morgan said.

"Well, I did tell you to take what you want," Adler said in a husky voice.

Morgan reached around her as Adler lifted herself away from the wall, enough to unclasp and remove her bra. Morgan stared at Adler's breasts only for a moment before she bent to take a nipple into her mouth and pressed Adler back against the wall. Adler's nipples were hard, too. Morgan knew she'd been the one to do that to her. That knowledge alone made the need between her own legs soar. She didn't have to worry, though, because Adler's hands were tugging at the sweats she'd put on after the shower. They were around her thighs by the time she moved to Adler's other nipple.

"What are you doing?" she asked.

"Taking your clothes off. I want to touch you," Adler replied.

Morgan let the nipple go with a pop. She raised her head to look into Adler's eyes. Clearly, this woman not only wanted to be touched by her, but she wanted to touch Morgan as well. The desire in the Adler's eyes said most of that. The fact that she was sliding her hand inside Morgan's underwear said the rest.

"Oh, God." Morgan's forehead went to Adler's shoulder.

"Touch me, too," Adler said.

Her fingers danced in Morgan's wetness. They were aimless for several strokes, but that didn't matter. Adler was touching her skin. She was stroking her most intimate parts. Morgan yanked down hard on Adler's jeans, needing more of her. Once they were down to her knees, she noticed Adler's matching lilac panties. They had a soft satin feel with a lace trim that had Morgan's mouth watering at the sight. Of course, that might have had something to do with the fact that the lilac was darker in one particular location. Morgan pulled them down to meet Adler's jeans. Adler's fingers finally started stroking her clit. She was soft and tentative, but it had Morgan ready to come all the same.

"Addie, you'll make me–"

"Touch me, Morgan. Please. I need you again."

"I want something else," Morgan said before kissing her.

Then, she slid her fingers back into Adler's wetness, moved them down lower, and entered her.

"Oh, yes," Adler breathed out. "Yes."

Morgan moved in and out slowly as Adler continued to stroke her. When Adler flicked her clit in just the right way, Morgan used her free hand to press the woman further into the wall at her shoulder, and pressed her own center over Adler's thigh again to apply more pressure and thrust into Adler harder.

"Addie, yes."

Morgan rode out her orgasm while searching deeper inside Adler to find the place that would make her come. Her free hand moved to Adler's breast. She clasped a nipple between her thumb and forefinger, tweaked it gently but enough to make Adler whimper again. She used her thumb to flick Adler's clit while her fingers curled inside the woman.

"Yes, yes." Adler's hips moved into her hand. "There. Yes."

Adler rocked against Morgan's hand as Morgan continued to rock into Adler's hand and thigh, riding out the embers of her own orgasm. When Morgan finally came down, her forehead was pressed to Adler's shoulder again. Adler's was doing the same on Morgan's shoulder. They were both breathing hard. Morgan could feel the sweat on her back and her brow. Her fingers remained inside Adler. Morgan stroked her inside slowly because she didn't want to not be inside Adler just yet.

"You are so good at this," she said to Adler when she finally caught her breath.

"I am?" Adler asked with a light laugh that reverberated against Morgan's shoulder.

"Oh, yeah." Morgan gave a light laugh back.

"Is it wrong that I want more?" Adler asked.

Morgan pulled back to look at her. Adler's eyes were still dark with need. Morgan used her thumb to feel Adler's still hard and swollen clit. She swirled her fingers around inside her and watched as Adler twitched. Yes, Adler had come, but her body still needed more. That worked out well for Morgan because she could give more. Morgan could give so much more to this woman she'd fallen so hard in love with, just feeling that twitch at her own fingers nearly brought her to happy tears.

CHAPTER 16

ADLER pushed back a little at Morgan now that her legs finally remembered how to walk. She needed her own back to not be pressed up against that wall anymore. She also needed to not be standing. Her hands were around Morgan's neck. Her lips were on Morgan's. Before she knew it, she had them both moved to the floor in front of the fireplace. Morgan was beneath her. She wasn't even sure how it had happened. She'd never experienced this before. Sex with her previous partners hadn't allowed her to get out of her head like this. With Morgan, it was like she had no control over her own body or mind. It was the best feeling she'd ever experienced. She wanted to allow herself to be consumed by Morgan Burns. Her lips moved to Morgan's neck. She could feel Morgan's hands gripping her ass, encouraging her to rock into her. She realized then that she must have kicked off her jeans, because she was naked. Morgan was naked, too. Their bodies were pressed fully together for the first time, and it still wasn't enough. Adler moved her thigh between Morgan's legs, pressed into her sex, and rocked as she lowered her lips to Morgan's breasts.

"Jesus, Addie!"

Morgan's hands pressed further into her, encouraging her to take her own pleasure against Morgan's thigh. She rocked harder, sliding her wetness over Morgan's leg.

"I want you," Adler said.

"You have me. I'm here. Take whatever you want."

"I want all of you," Adler corrected. "All of it, Morgan." She looked up to meet Morgan's eyes. "I've never felt—"

Morgan took Adler's hand, slid it between her own

legs, and said, "Addie, all of me already belongs to you. Take it. Claim it."

Adler slid two fingers inside Morgan, groaning at the feel of the softness that enveloped her own fingers. She roamed deeper. She was inside a woman. Her fingers were responsible for the hips that were rising beneath her. Morgan's orgasm came so quickly, Adler hadn't been prepared for it. She watched the expression on Morgan's face. She continued to thrust inside her until the hips stopped entirely. Morgan's body stiffened and then relaxed completely.

She watched as Morgan opened her amazing eyes. She appeared to be sated, but something told Adler, Morgan Burns really *could* go all night. Adler pulled her fingers out, sliding them up to Morgan's clit instead. She stroked her gently and slowly. She watched Morgan climb again to another climax. Then, she pressed her body fully against the woman beneath her. Morgan's breathing slowed to normal within a few moments. Adler wondered if she'd been wrong: maybe Morgan had fallen asleep. Before she could lift herself up to check, Morgan had rolled her over and was now on top of her.

Both women were covered in a thin sheen of sweat thanks to their activities as well as the proximity to the still burning fire. Morgan sucked on Adler's nipples, one after the other. Then, she kissed her abdomen, smirking at the twitching muscles beneath her lips. Adler realized where Morgan was headed. She spread her legs wide, watched Morgan continue to kiss, lick, and suck at her flesh, and enjoyed the anticipation of what was to come. Morgan kissed the inside of both of her thighs. She looked up with those blue eyes Adler loved, and licked her without asking for permission or if Adler was sure. Adler's hips bucked immediately. Morgan didn't need any more coaxing than that. Her hands held on to the outside of Adler's thighs. She took her fully into her mouth.

"That's..." Adler watched Morgan work between her legs. "So good. That's so good. Don't stop."

Morgan didn't stop. Her lips engulfed Adler's clit. She sucked and sucked until Adler's hand went to the back of her head. Adler pressed Morgan even harder against her. Morgan's head bobbed up and down while her tongue flicked against swollen flesh. Then, Adler's eyes closed. Her hips rose. Everything went blank. Her orgasm rocketed through every part of her as Morgan took what she wanted. She screamed. She didn't moan or groan. She didn't say Morgan's name under her breath. She screamed it. Morgan didn't stop. She slid her fingers inside Adler. Adler hadn't even come down yet, and she was coming again already. Morgan moaned against her. She continued to thrust and suck until Adler screamed again and collapsed against the floor.

***

"I love this," Morgan said minutes later.

Adler was lying on her stomach. Morgan had her hand in the woman's hair. They were still nude. The fire had almost died completely. Their hearts had returned to their normal rate. Their wineglasses were empty. Morgan's body was pleasantly sore. She was certain Adler's was, too. She'd always believed she'd had great sex in her day, but… God, being with this woman, being with Adler, was the best experience she'd had in her life. She wasn't just including sex. It was the best thing she'd ever done. Summiting a mountain, tackling class IV rapids, opening her first store after her parents retired – none of that compared to how it felt having this woman touch her.

"Me too," Adler mumbled against her skin.

"Tired?" Morgan asked.

"A little," Adler said.

"Sore?"

"A lot," she said and laughed. "But that doesn't have to mean we're done for the night."

Morgan laughed then and replied, "It's only ten. We could take this up to the bedroom."

"That sounds amazing. Any chance the bedroom can come to us, though?" Adler asked.

"I don't think so, Addie." Morgan sat up, displacing Adler from her body.

"Hey," Adler said.

"Come on. I'll get the wine bottle from the kitchen. You grab the glasses. I'll meet you in the bathroom, where we will get into that nice, deep bathtub I have. We'll run some hot water. You can lie back against me."

"That also sounds amazing," Adler agreed, leaned forward, and kissed her.

They made it upstairs a few minutes later. Morgan poured the rest of the wine into their glasses. Adler started the bath. Morgan watched as the woman stretched her tired limbs. Suddenly, Morgan was wide awake. All of her, every part of her, woke up at the sight of Adler Williams standing naked in her bathroom, sipping on a glass of red wine. She smiled softly at the woman who caught her eye.

"What?" Adler asked.

"Nothing. You're just really hot."

"Says the woman with the flat-as-fuck abs." She pointed at Morgan.

"I don't have any problems with your abs." Morgan moved to her, placed Adler's wineglass on the counter, and ran her fingers along Adler's abdomen. "Perfect."

"You can't do that right now. You know how I go from zero to sixty," Adler said in that sexy, husky voice.

"I love how you go from zero to sixty," Morgan replied, kissing her neck. "And you told me to take what I want."

"What is it you want right now?"

"Just you. Again." Morgan nipped at Adler's neck.

"Let's make a deal: I will let you do whatever you want to me…"

"That's the best deal I've ever heard," Morgan said against Adler's skin.

"That's only part one, Morgan." She gave Morgan a

light shove backward. "But I get to take what I want, too." She kissed Morgan's lips. "And I get to go first."

"Deal," Morgan replied as she was pressed against the counter.

Adler smirked at her. Then, she knelt in front of her. She nudged Morgan's thighs apart. Morgan watched as Adler looked up at her, settled into her position, and then softly licked the inside of her thigh. Morgan gasped at that first touch. She could hear the water running in the bathtub behind them. Then, she could hear nothing as Adler sucked her into her mouth. Adler moaned. Morgan moaned. Then, Morgan's hips were moving. Her hands were on the back of Adler's head. She opened her eyes and watched the woman, who was on her knees, making a woman come with her mouth for the first time. Morgan loved that she was Adler's *first.* She prayed silently, as Adler flicked the tip of her tongue against her clit, that she'd be her *only.* Morgan came with her eyes open, still watching as Adler looked up at her with a smile on her face.

"Are you?" the woman asked before resuming her ministrations.

"Yes, don't stop. Addie, fuck."

Morgan rode out her orgasm as her hips pressed further into Adler's face. When she slowed, Adler's strokes did, too. Then, Adler kissed her clit once, twice, and again, causing tremors to overtake Morgan.

"Again?" Adler asked, applying another kiss.

"After."

"After what?" Adler asked.

"After my turn," Morgan said.

***

Adler's eyes were open as she took in Morgan's light skin against the dark blue of the comforter. Morgan had fallen asleep hours earlier. Adler had, too, technically. She'd woken to grab much-needed water. Then, she'd returned to their shared bed, still naked, as was Morgan. Adler could only stare at her. She knew if she touched Morgan, she'd be on fire again. It took nothing to get her going where this woman was concerned. She wondered if that meant she'd been wrong about herself all along. Had she been gay and finally just figured it out? Was she still straight, but loved Morgan's touch? Did it really matter?

She could probably spend hours talking to Paxton about this. Paxton had come out as a teenager. She'd told Adler that she'd always known she was attracted to women. She'd never wanted to be with a man. Adler, however, had never felt attracted to a woman. She'd always been interested in the opposite sex. She'd blamed her failed relationships on either the work or the men themselves. She'd heard so many times that the amount of time she spent at work was too much. She didn't have enough left over to dedicate to a relationship. That was probably true, but it said something that she preferred time at work to time with her boyfriends more often than not.

She knew that part of her would likely not change. She'd always been ambitious. That kind of drive took a lot of time. As she stared at Morgan, though, she wondered how the hell they'd be able to do this. Morgan was just as busy as she was. They'd managed texts every day and phone calls whenever they could, but that was when they were only friends. Adler didn't know what they were to one another officially, but she knew they were more than friends now. She knew she wanted to see Morgan every day. She also knew that, at least in the immediate future, that wasn't possible.

Adler had to return home. Her job was there. Her apartment was there. Her sister was there. Her parents, that she didn't see all that often, were there, too. Morgan had her life here. She'd just bought a house. Her business was headquartered here. She was about to open a new store in Jackson Hole, but she'd still reside in South Lake Tahoe. How often would they be able to talk? How many times a month could they even see each other? Adler was lucky: her salary was enough to more than survive on in the city. She also had some money saved up. They could do weekends, maybe. The flights weren't that long.

"I can hear you thinking all the way over here," Morgan mumbled.

"I thought you were asleep," Adler whispered and scooted closer to her.

"I was. I woke up. Why are you awake?" Morgan rolled onto her back.

"I thought you could go all night," Adler remarked, running two fingers down Morgan's stomach to between her legs. She needed to avoid all the scenarios running through her head right now. The best way to do that was to touch Morgan. "I woke up wanting you again."

"You did?" Morgan asked as Adler's fingers slid between her folds. "It's five in the morning, Addie. You are definitely a morning person." The woman chuckled until Adler began stroking her. "And I'm really okay with that."

CHAPTER 17

"YOU two are together now?" Kinsley asked.

"We haven't talked specifics, but... yeah, we are."

"And you guys have..."

"Yes, James; we've had sex." Morgan rolled her eyes at her friend. "And sex, and sex, and sex." She smiled wistfully at the memory. "It's been three days of that and food in between, to keep our energy up. Every muscle in my body hurts, and I am loving it."

Kinsley laughed and replied, "I think that's great, Morgan."

"You didn't want me to go there with her." Morgan turned to her friend.

"That's not true. I was just worried she *couldn't* be with you the way you so obviously wanted. Now, I don't have to worry about that. You two are obviously in that blissful honeymoon period."

Morgan looked toward Kinsley's backyard where she spotted Riley and Adler heading toward the boat Kinsley had restored. The two of them were already on board, organizing the stuff they'd brought for their day on the water. When she noticed that Adler was wearing her shorts and her bikini top only, her jaw dropped open.

"We are," Morgan replied to Kinsley's statement. "God, she's..."

"Let's just say we are both very lucky," Kinsley said.

Morgan turned to see that Kinsley was staring at her own girlfriend, who'd also chosen to only wear shorts and a bikini top to the boat.

"What are you two talking about?" Riley asked as she dropped her bag into the boat from the short dock.

113

"You two," Kinsley replied.

"What about us?" Adler asked Morgan.

"Terrible things, obviously," Morgan replied with a wink as she reached out to take Adler's hand, helping her into the boat. "Hi." She kissed the woman.

"Hi," Adler kissed Morgan back. "I like your friends," she whispered.

"They can hear you," Kinsley said with a laugh.

"I knew that," Adler whispered and offered Kinsley a smile. "Now, I am ready to go for a ride on the lake."

"Then, let's do this," Kinsley said.

"So, you like my friends?" Morgan asked, slinging her arm over Adler's back when they sat down on the back bench seat.

"I do. Riley's great. And I can see why you and Kinsley are such good friends." Adler then turned and whispered, "Nothing ever happened between you two, though, right? Just you and Reese?"

"Yes," Morgan replied. "Reese and I were friends for a long time before we started dating. Kinsley's been around for most of that, but nothing's ever been between us."

Kinsley had started the engine, thankfully. She and Riley were snuggled close as Kinsley steered the boat out into the water. Morgan took the opportunity to turn her face toward Adler and kiss her slowly at first. Her hand moved into Adler's hair, which she'd worn up, but the wisps were still heaven between Morgan's fingers. Adler's tongue joined Morgan's. Morgan let out a soft moan. Then, Adler's hand was on her thigh. It slid up and under the hem of Morgan's shorts, resting there. Adler pulled back and bit her lower lip.

"Okay… None of that," the woman said, pointing at Morgan with the hand that she'd only just removed from Morgan's thigh. "You know how I get."

"I just wanted to kiss you; *you* did the rest," Morgan argued.

"What is it with you? I've never been like this," Adler said, resting her head on Morgan's shoulder.

"I don't know." Morgan kissed the top of her head. "But this is the first time we've left the house in days. You're in one of the most beautiful places in the world, in my opinion; I want you to see it."

"I want to see you naked again," Adler whispered, lifting her head to do so.

"Trust me, you will." Morgan kissed her lips.

The boat continued its path on the lake for the next several minutes. Kinsley passed Riley the wheel and joined Adler and Morgan in the back. They talked and laughed until Riley stopped the boat. Then, they ate a late lunch together. Morgan enjoyed watching Adler with her friends. They all seemed to like one another. She also enjoyed that, for the first time in a long time, she had someone, too. She played with the ends of Adler's hair as Adler told Riley about her work. Kinsley sat between Riley's legs, resting back against her girlfriend. Morgan wondered what was next for those two. They'd been together for a while now. They lived together. It was only a matter of time before they got engaged, married, and started a family. Kellan and Reese would be married soon. She'd be Reese's maid of honor.

She looked over at Adler and wondered what the next step would be for them. Adler's vacation was over in a little more than a week. They'd already shared more than Morgan had ever hoped, but she didn't want it to stop here. She didn't want Adler to leave; she didn't want this vacation of amazing experiences to be the end of them. Her biggest fear, as she toyed with Adler's hair while watching her laugh at something Kinsley had said, was that she'd leave, time would get the better of them, and Adler would realize this thing between them wasn't worth the work. She'd be lying if she didn't add to that fear that she worried Adler might also not want to deal with the complication of being with a woman.

"You okay?" Adler turned to ask her.

"I'm good. You?" she asked.

"Never been better," Adler said with a smile. She

kissed Morgan gently on the lips. "Now, I've never been better."

"Are you two going to game night tonight?" Kinsley asked.

"Game night?" Adler asked Morgan.

"At Reese and Kellan's place," Riley added. "They do one of these every so often. Everyone will be there."

"I think Stacy is out of town again. She seems to always be working these days. But everyone else will be there," Kinsley said.

"Stacy and her husband have been friends with Reese, Remy, and me since forever. We all grew up together."

"So, Remy and Ryan will be there?" Adler asked.

"Yup." Morgan kissed her cheek. "You'll get to meet everyone."

"Well, except Morgan's parents. They won't be there," Kinsley said with a playful smirk.

"James…" Morgan warned.

"Are we at the meet the parents stage?" Adler asked. "If so, I'm in."

"You want to meet my parents?" Morgan laughed.

"Sure. Why not? I'm here. If you don't want to introduce me as your girlfriend, that's okay. I–" Adler's eyes went wide.

"I'd happily introduce you as my girlfriend." Morgan kissed her cheek. "But, to meet my parents, you'd have to go to them."

"Okay. Where are they?"

Morgan pointed out into the woods and replied, "Out there somewhere."

***

"I'm sorry about the whole parents-thing on the boat." Adler snuggled into Morgan's side as they approached Kellan and Reese's house.

"Why?"

"Well, first, I called myself your girlfriend, when we

haven't even talked about that stuff yet. Then, I told you I wanted to meet your parents in front of your friends. That's something we should talk about the timing of. I shouldn't have just blurted it out like that."

"Addie, my parents aren't like regular parents. They're a bit eccentric. I guess they always have been, in a way. But since they retired, sold their house, and now basically camp full-time either here or at other state and national parks all over the country, they're even more eccentric. They don't care that I'm gay. They never have. I've only ever introduced Reese to them as my girlfriend. I'm sure they'd be happy to see me with someone else after all this time."

"And I'm about to meet this Reese. Anything I should know before we go inside?" Adler asked.

"Just that I am absolutely going to introduce you as my hot girlfriend." Morgan kissed her and rang the doorbell at the same time. "And that you have nothing to worry about. I don't have feelings for Reese anymore."

"Hey, Mo. This must be Adler... I'm Reese." The woman smiled upon opening the door. "Come on in. Remy's already talking smack about Monopoly. I thought we'd start with Scrabble, though."

"As long as we're not playing Risk," Morgan replied, hugging her friend. "And yes, this is my girlfriend, Adler." She pulled on Adler's hand to bring her into the house. "Let's maybe slowly get her used to how ridiculously competitive you are, instead of all at once, okay? I'm trying to keep her."

Adler smiled at Morgan's comment and said, "It's nice to meet you."

"You too. Come on in. Kell's in the kitchen. James and Riley are already out back."

Morgan pulled again at Adler's hand toward the open kitchen, where she found Kellan taking the caps off several beer bottles.

"Kell, this is Adler." She motioned to her right. "My hot girlfriend."

"Nice to meet you, Adler, the hot girlfriend." Kellan laughed. "And did my hot fiancée just run back outside without helping me with these beers?"

"Yes, yes, she did." Morgan moved into the kitchen. "I'll grab us each one and help with the rest."

"Thank you." She looked at Adler. "And it really is nice to meet you. This one wouldn't stop talking about you for months."

"Kellan!"

"Really?" Adler asked her.

"Constantly," a woman, who looked just like Reese but with a different hair color, said from the living room as she made her way toward the kitchen. "She's been very annoying lately." She winked at Morgan. "I'm going to the bathroom before we get started." She looked back at Adler. "I'm Remy. It's nice to meet you."

"You too." Adler shook the hand Remy held out for her.

"Bathroom," Remy said with a smile and walked off.

"We're a strange group, but we're family." Morgan wrapped her arm around Adler's waist. "Are you sure you want to go out back? It's going to get crazy."

"I'm sure." Adler laughed.

They made their way out to a screened-in porch with a nice sunset view of the wilderness behind the house. Adler made the rounds and was introduced to the rest of the group. They all sat around a giant picnic table. The first game was Monopoly. There were two boards set out on the table. Adler sat at one. Morgan at the other. They followed standard Monopoly rules to make the games go faster. When two people won, they played each other to determine the winner for the night. Adler had won her game and had to play Remy for the final victory. Unfortunately, Morgan sat next to her for this game and had taken to applying slow, circular strokes on Adler's lower back under her shirt. Adler never stood a chance. Scrabble came next. Morgan and Adler both lost, but they enjoyed the trash talk around the group. When Morgan went into the kitchen to grab another beer, Adler followed.

"Can I talk to you outside, please?" she asked, walking quickly to the front door of the house without waiting for a response.

"Is everything okay?" Morgan asked. "Addie?" Morgan half-yelled.

Adler made her way toward the car and waited for Morgan to arrive.

CHAPTER 18

"ADDIE, what the hell happened? Are you okay?" Morgan asked, meeting her at the back of the car.

"No, I'm not okay. You cost me a victory in there; you know that."

"What?" Morgan questioned.

Adler pressed Morgan into the back of the car and said, "You were touching me. You know how I get when you touch me."

"Oh," Morgan replied. "Really?"

"Yes, really." Adler unbuttoned her jeans. She watched Morgan lick her lips and lower her gaze as she slid the zipper down. "They're all inside."

Morgan turned them around swiftly, pinning Adler to the car instead. She slid her thigh between Adler's legs and her hand inside Adler's panties.

"You're soaked," Morgan said.

"Your fault," Adler replied with a smile.

"I should probably make it up to you, then," Morgan suggested.

She stroked Adler quickly, not wanting to waste any time.

"Hey, Morgan!" Kinsley's voice came from the front porch. "Reese is thinking about getting Risk going. I need your vote to overrule her."

Morgan stopped her movements. Adler resisted the urge to growl. Morgan slid her hand out of Adler's pants, kissed her softly, and then slid her coated fingers into Adler's mouth. Adler sucked on them, causing Morgan's own wetness to pool. Then, Morgan pulled her fingers away.

"Coming."

"I'm not," Adler said under her breath as she buttoned up her pants.

**

"She's great, Mo."

"I think so," Morgan replied.

She and Reese were sitting on the front porch swing while the rest of the group played charades inside the house.

"So, you guys are official?"

"We are. She called herself my girlfriend. I want her to be my girlfriend."

"And you're not worried about the distance or the fact that you're the only woman she's ever been with?"

"Damn, Reese. You could ease into the deep stuff," Morgan said and took a drink of her beer.

"Could I? Game night's wrapping up, and I've hardly seen you recently."

"She's only here for two weeks. I–"

"You don't need to explain yourself to me, Morgan." Reese turned to her. "I know what it's like to want to spend every free moment with someone. I also know what it's like when that person doesn't live here."

Morgan nodded at the recollection of how Reese and Kellan started dating. Kellan had been on vacation in Tahoe and called San Francisco home back then.

"That's a little different, though."

"How so?" Reese asked.

"Kellan moved here right after you two started. She didn't really have anything keeping her in San Francisco. She took over Dr. Sanders' vet practice when he retired. She's actually living her dream here in Tahoe: she got you and her dream job."

"And you don't think Adler can have that?"

"She already has her dream job. It's in Seattle. She also has her family there. I'm the only thing she has here."

"Are you worried she won't ever want to move here if you guys continue dating?"

"I guess, yeah."

"Would you ever move to Seattle?" Reese asked.

"I couldn't even if I wanted to," Morgan replied, finishing her beer.

"The business?"

"Not just that. You know how I get in cities… That's not the life for me."

"Is this the life for her?"

"I don't know. She hated camping when I first met her. But, now, she seems to like it."

"Camping is a vacation or a weekend away, Mo. Does she like Tahoe? Would she like living here; having a house here with you one day; making a family, if that's what you two decide you want? Could she give up living in a big city like that and move to what basically amounts to a tourist trap most of the year? It's a beautiful tourist trap that I love, but our town is no major city."

"Trust me, I'm well aware."

"And?"

"And I don't know. I knew I wanted to be with her when I first met her. But this is still so new, Reese. I never thought she'd return my feelings. Just knowing that she does is enough for now."

"If it's enough for now, then I think that's all that matters." Reese placed her hand on top of Morgan's. "I want you to be so happy, Morgan."

"I know. Me too. For you, I mean."

"I am," Reese replied with a smile. "I'm marrying Kellan in a few months. We're going to start trying to have kids after we get back from our honeymoon. I love my job, my friends, and my family. I have what I want in my life. I just want to make sure you have the same."

"Hey, I think the fun is breaking up," Adler said when she opened the front door. "Oh, hi." She nodded at Reese, who removed her hand from Morgan's. "Remy and Ryan are about to leave. Kinsley and Riley said they were right behind them."

"Okay. We can head out," Morgan said and stood. "Let me just grab my stuff." She kissed Adler's cheek and headed inside, closing the door behind her.

***

"Thanks for coming out tonight. It was a lot of fun having you here," Reese told her.

"Thanks for the invite," Adler replied, locking her hands together in front of herself.

Reese stood and said, "Is it weird?"

"Because you used to sleep with my girlfriend?" Adler asked. "Yes, it's a little weird."

"There's nothing between us anymore. I'm engaged to Kellan; she has you."

"I know. I believe you both." Adler shrugged.

"But it's still weird?" Reese asked.

"You two have a very long history, from what she's told me. Plus, I leave in a few days, and you'll still be here."

"Morgan's very important to me. She's always been in my life, and I hope she always will be, but I won't ever get in the way of her happiness. From what I've seen, you make her pretty happy." Reese looked through the front window at Morgan, who was hugging Kinsley good night. "And from what I've seen, she makes you pretty happy, too."

"She does." Adler smiled. "I thought I was crazy, at first. When I met her, I was on an anniversary trip with my *boyfriend*. He'd planned this camping thing as a surprise. I spent the entire time complaining until he finally couldn't put up with it anymore and took us to a hotel. When I saw her, though, I was completely taken." She looked into the window to see Morgan hugging Riley with a wide smile on her face. "She said something about how camping can be great when you're with the right person. I spent the night outside with her, staring at the beautiful mountains and the sunset before the moon and stars. I kept stealing glances at her, though, and I couldn't help but think she was even more beautiful than all of that combined."

"That's a pretty big deal." Reese smiled at her.

"*She* is a pretty big deal. She's not just my first girl-friend, Reese. I think she might be my only. I just don't want to screw this up."

"Why would you do that?"

"It's not easy being in a long-distance relationship. Truthfully, I missed her even when we were just friends. Now, it's going to be worse."

"But, be honest with yourself, Adler: were you two ever *just* friends?" Reese asked, placing her hand on Adler's forearm. "Sounds to me like it was always more than that for both of you."

The door opened. The game night participants came flooding out. Kellan stood in the doorway. Reese moved to join her. Riley and Kinsley each offered her a hug before Remy and Ryan took their turn. Then, she caught Morgan hugging Reese goodbye. It was a sweet, friendly hug shared between the women that had known one another forever. When Morgan reached for Adler's hand blindly, without finishing the hug, Adler took it and squeezed it. Morgan and Reese separated. Morgan turned to look at her, kissed her on the cheek, and smiled.

"Are you ready?" Morgan asked. Adler nodded. She said thanks to Kellan and Reese for allowing her into their home. Then, she said goodbye to the rest of the group as everyone piled into their cars. "Would you mind driving? I had a few beers. I want to be safe," Morgan said and passed her the keys.

"No problem."

Adler climbed behind the wheel. Morgan sat in the passenger's seat. After another round of waving from the car, Adler backed them out of the driveway, and they joined the minuscule amount of traffic on the main road. Morgan ran her hand through her hair as she stared at her girlfriend who, apparently, already knew her way home. She smiled at that thought. Before she thought too much about the fact that it wasn't technically Adler's home, she leaned over and unbuttoned Adler's jeans.

"What are you doing?" Adler asked.

"Getting my revenge."

Morgan slid inside Adler's underwear with ease. Adler even moved her hips forward a little to allow her access. Morgan smirked at how much Adler wanted this. She stroked her girlfriend slowly, until the car came to a stop at a light. Then, she moved two fingers faster against Adler's swollen clit. Adler's eyes closed as her head flew back against the headrest. Morgan leaned over further and kissed Adler's neck. She pressed her hand fully into Adler's sex, allowing the woman to rock her hips into it, applying more pressure.

"I needed this," Adler said as she opened her eyes and looked over at Morgan. "Don't stop until I come."

"Oh, I won't."

The light must have turned green, because Adler's attention returned to the road, and the car sped off.

"There." Adler pressed one hand on top of Morgan's. "Yes, there."

Adler thrusted her own pelvis a little harder and came against Morgan's hand with a few expletives. Morgan kissed her neck a few more times, toyed with her earlobe, and continued to stroke her clit until Adler finally came all the way down. Then, Morgan's phone buzzed in her pocket.

"At least it's *after* your orgasm."

She picked up the phone and stared at the screen. It was a text from Kinsley. Morgan looked over at the lane next to them to see Riley behind the wheel and Kinsley in the passenger's seat. Kinsley smirked at her and gave her a thumbs-up.

"What's wrong?" Adler asked.

"Oh, nothing. My friends are just in the lane next to us. And they totally saw me get you off while we're driving."

CHAPTER 19

TWO days later, Adler was sitting in Morgan's back-yard watching the sunset behind the tall pine trees. She had a glass of wine resting on the table next to her chair. She also had Morgan kneeling in front of her, making her come with her mouth.

"I love how you taste," Morgan said and went back to work.

"I love how you do that," Adler replied, playing with Morgan's hair. "And that," she added when Morgan flicked her clit with the tongue. "Oh, and that, too. That. Yes, that."

Morgan moved faster. Her head bobbed up and down underneath Adler's dress. She couldn't see her girlfriend's face, but she knew she was smiling. They'd gone to a nice dinner at a lakefront restaurant that night. Afterward, they'd come back home and poured the wine, opting to take it out-side to enjoy the rest of the sunset. Adler had sat down next to Morgan, with the table between them. They'd held hands in silence. It was a perfect moment. Then, Morgan made it even more perfect by sliding her finger up and down Adler's forearm. It hadn't taken much more than that. Within minutes, Morgan had gotten to her knees, pulled off Adler's panties, spread her legs, and took her.

"That was nice," Morgan said, removing her head from under Adler's dress, wiping her mouth and standing.

"That was really nice," Adler replied, pulling Morgan into her. She pressed her face to Morgan's stomach and breathed her in. "Hey, do you think we can do that sunrise canoe thing we were going to do when we went camping before I go?"

"Sure, if you want to wake up early and head out," Morgan said, running her fingers through Adler's hair. "What made you think of that?"

"I don't know… I guess I've just gotten used to watching sunrises and sunsets with you. I wouldn't mind adding one more to the list." Adler kissed through Morgan's shirt.

"Tomorrow morning?" Morgan asked.

"Only if we get to bed soon." Adler lifted Morgan's shirt and kissed her again. "This chair is the kind that lays flat, isn't it?" She kissed Morgan's skin again just above her navel.

"It does lie flat, yes." Morgan chuckled. "Why do you ask?"

"Make it go down for me?"

Morgan moved around her girlfriend, pulled at the chair, and watched as Adler and the chair lowered.

"There you go. Now, what's going on in that head of yours?"

"You wore a skirt tonight," Adler stated. "I've never seen you in a skirt. You're hot in a skirt." She sat up and pulled Morgan toward her. Then, she reached under Morgan's skirt and pulled down her underwear. "Come here." Adler lay back down and encouraged Morgan to straddle her hips.

"I'm going to make a mess on that pretty dress." Morgan pointed at her.

"Then, lift my dress up."

Morgan reached for the hem of the knee-length dress. She lifted it up, revealing Adler's skin beneath, and climbed on top of her girlfriend, straddling her hips. She rocked slowly into her as Adler held on to her waist.

"Now, what should I do?" Morgan asked with a smirk.

"You should do what I did to you the other night," Adler said while encouraging Morgan to rock faster.

"Sit on your face?" Morgan asked. "Addie, are–"

"Morgan, stop," Adler said. "I can feel how wet you are. I want to taste you. Come up here."

Morgan lifted her skirt a little more and slid up Adler's body. She rested her knees on either side of Adler's head. Then, she lowered herself. Adler gripped her hips and lowered her even more. Her tongue touched Morgan first. When it did, Morgan's body – that had been coiled so tight from the sensations of bringing Adler to climax – started to let go. Her hips rocked against Adler's mouth. Adler moaned. She sucked on Morgan's clit. Before she could even think of what to do next, Morgan was rocking harder. Adler realized she didn't need to do anything. Morgan would take what she wanted. Adler would benefit. When Morgan ground herself harder, Adler felt the woman shift above her. Morgan's fingers found purchase between Adler's legs. Adler moaned when Morgan stroked her while rocking against her face. They came together, with Morgan's hips still twitching every now and then, just as Adler's hips did when Morgan stroked her slowly.

"Wow," Morgan said. She lifted herself up and slid back down to Adler's hips. "That was really, really good."

"Yes, you were." Adler winked at her. "Now, I think we can take a shower and get some sleep. I want to wake up early with you tomorrow and see the sunrise over Lake Tahoe."

***

Morgan woke Adler with a kiss on the shoulder the following morning.

"Hi," Adler said.

"Do you still want to see the sunrise?"

"Is it time?" Adler asked, kissing Morgan softly on the lips.

"We've got about an hour. But we need to get to the boat and get out on the water."

"Let's go, then," Adler said with another kiss.

They dressed slowly. Adler made them both coffee and packed it in thermoses so that they could enjoy it later. Morgan packed a bag. They dressed in layers to keep warm.

Then, they drove the short distance to where Morgan's store had a canoe rental outpost. She unlocked everything with her own key and pulled out the boat and oars. They settled everything in the canoe. Then, they pushed it out and climbed inside. The boat rocked a little, but they managed not to tip it over.

They rowed, looking at each other in between glances at the scenery that was slowly starting to show itself as the morning came. Morgan stopped rowing after several minutes, and Adler put her own oar down. They floated there for a while, looking at one another and sharing small talk and coffee. When the sun started rising in the sky, Adler watched the dark browns and navy blues turn to purples, oranges, and pinks. She glanced at her girlfriend, who was doing the same. Then, she reached for Morgan's hand. Morgan took her hand into her own, rubbing her thumb over Adler's knuckles while her baby blues stared into Adler's eyes. Adler swallowed. She remembered the real reason why she'd wanted to come out here this morning.

"I love you," she said softly.

Morgan's eyes went big. Her thumb stopped moving. Adler was terrified she'd made the wrong decision.

"I love you, too, Addie." Morgan appeared to let out a deep breath. "I love you, too."

***

"I told her, Pax," Adler said to her sister.

"You told her you love her?"

"We were on the water at sunrise. I told her. She said she loves me, too. It was perfect."

"I'm happy for you, sis," Paxton said. "Oh, I'm thinking about having some people over at my place on Saturday. You're back on Friday, aren't you?"

Adler closed her eyes and said, "Yes, I fly back on Friday."

"Then, you better be there."

"Sure, Pax."

"Hey, what's wrong? You were so happy a minute ago."

Adler was lying on the beach. There were people everywhere. It definitely wasn't as private here as the beach she and Morgan had been on when she'd first arrived. God, that seemed like so long ago. Had it really been less than two weeks ago? Morgan was in the water. Her girlfriend was technically working today. She was teaching one of her new employees how to tie up the kayaks. She was also wearing shorts and her bikini top. She was gorgeous.

"I'm leaving," Adler said to her sister on the phone.

"Oh. I'm sorry, Adler. You knew that going in, though."

"I did. But I had no idea what I'd be leaving behind then," Adler replied as she watched Morgan tie one kayak to another.

"What are you guys going to do?" Paxton asked.

"I don't know. We still haven't talked about it. I think we're both avoiding it on purpose."

"You can't do that for much longer."

"I know, Pax. I know." Adler lowered her head to her blanket and stared at the sky. "I'm going to miss her like crazy."

"Think of it like this: if you're at home, you're usually so busy with work, you don't have any time left over to miss her."

"I don't even think work will get my mind off her. It didn't before. I used to text her every free moment I had. In between meetings, I'd send her lame emojis if I didn't have time for a real message."

Paxton laughed and replied, "None of that has to change. You'll find moments to do lame crap like that, to talk on the phone, video chat, and other stuff."

"Other stuff?"

"Yeah, Adler. You'll be in a long-distance relationship. *Other stuff.*"

Adler sat up quickly and whispered, "Are you talking about phone sex?"

"I am." Paxton laughed again. "Have you gotten her stance on that yet?"

"We haven't even talked about the fact that I'm leaving."

"So, no. Got it. Well, I'd add that to the list. Talk about who's taking the next trip to see the other person. I assume her, since you're there right now. Talk about when that could possibly happen. If you can, you should book it while you're there. It'll make you both feel better, knowing you have a trip back to each other planned."

"And talk about phone sex?"

"I would. Well, I did. When I dated Becky for six months after she moved to Denver, she and I–"

"Nope. I don't want to know." Adler covered her eyes as if that would protect her from hearing about her sister's sex life.

"Excuse me. I had to hear about you and Little Miss Tahoe over there."

"Paxton, please forgive me for making you listen to me talk about my sex life with Morgan."

"Forgiven." Paxton sighed. "Talk to her, Adler. You guys need to come up with a plan if this thing between you has any chance of working."

"I know. You're right."

"And I want to meet this girl. I've never really cared about any of the guys you dated, because it didn't seem like any of those relationships were going anywhere. This one, though, seems like it might."

"I hope so." Adler smiled.

"Then, I definitely need to meet her. Tell her to come for a visit soon, okay? I need to do the sister dinner thing where I threaten her life if she ever hurts you."

"You don't need to do that," Adler replied while shaking her head at her sister.

"Adler, tell me the truth, okay?" Paxton got suddenly serious.

"Okay."

"Is she the one?" she asked.

Adler looked at Morgan, who was walking toward her with a smile on her face. Morgan was shaking a spray can of sunscreen at her. She then looked Adler up and down, wiggling her eyebrows.

"Have you re-applied since you got out of the water?" Morgan asked as she sat down next to her on the beach blanket.

"The answer to your question is yes, Paxton." She kissed Morgan's cheek. "I've got to go. Morgan's going to apply my sunscreen."

CHAPTER 20

"MY name is Adler Williams, and I'm an addict," Adler said.

Morgan laughed wildly and replied, "Yeah? What exactly are you addicted to?"

"You." Adler kissed Morgan's hipbone. "I am definitely addicted to you."

"I love you, Addie." Morgan ran her hand through Adler's hair. "What are we going to do?"

"I guess it's time for this conversation, huh?" Adler asked as she kissed up Morgan's stomach, sucked on a nipple briefly, and then kissed her collarbone.

"I guess so. It's your last night here."

"Don't say that." Adler lifted up to look down at her girlfriend. "It sounds really bad when you say it like that."

"It's our reality, Addie. You have a flight at one in the afternoon tomorrow. I don't know when I'll see you after that." Morgan kissed her hard. "I'm going to miss you so much."

"Let's figure it out, then," Adler replied and sat up to straddle Morgan's hips.

"Figure what out?"

"When you'll see me again. Can you come to Seattle?"

"When?"

"Morgan, any time. Come to Seattle the first chance you get."

"I'm going back to Wyoming next weekend, to sign the papers for the store."

"The next weekend?" Adler asked.

"I'm supposed to go to North Lake to spend time with my parents. They're parking their RV there for a few days before they leave for Yosemite."

"The weekend after?" Adler pressed.

"Jackson Hole again, to meet with the contractor."

"You're just as busy as I am," Adler said as she slid to Morgan's side.

"The weekend after, I'm free. Are you?"

"I will be, if it means I get to see you," Adler said, turning on her side toward Morgan.

"I'll book my flight after you leave, then," Morgan said and kissed her.

"Can we book it tonight?" Adler asked.

"Tonight? Sure. Why?"

"Something my sister said about booking things so you know they're actually happening," Adler replied. "And I can come back here after that."

"When?" Morgan asked.

"Let me get my phone."

"I'll get my computer," Morgan said.

She stood and walked naked out of the room. Adler reached for her phone and pulled up her calendar. Morgan then came back and sat back on the bed to sign onto her computer. As she brought up the site to book her flight, Adler scrolled forward to the next month, to see when she'd be available to come back to Tahoe.

"I think we should be smart about this. Technically, I have a board meeting, and I always get slammed with work after that. The next few weekends I'd be too busy to come, but I could come the weekend after."

"Wait, slow down. Explain that to me again." Morgan turned to her.

"If you come in a month, I'll come the next month."

"One month apart?" Morgan asked.

"I think it makes the most sense. I'll come here the following month. We can plan the next few trips after that," Adler suggested.

"This sucks, Addie. I don't want to be away from you for a month at a time," Morgan said, entering her login information and searching for flights.

"It's just the preliminary plan. We can talk about it more later."

"I know. I just... I'm going to miss you," Morgan said.

"Me too." Adler leaned over and kissed Morgan's knee. "I love you, though. We'll make this work." She kissed her thigh. "Morgan, this is the first time I've ever really cared enough to work at a relationship. It might make me sound like a bad person, but it's the truth. I'll come here as often as I can."

"And I'll go there as often as I can."

"I think that's the best we can do for now."

"I guess so," Morgan replied.

***

"I love you," Adler said as she kissed her.

"I love you, too," Morgan replied.

She tried to hold back the tears that were forming in her eyes. She knew it was no use. Adler wiped them off her cheeks as they fell. Morgan sniffled as they stood inside the airport in front of security. Morgan held on to Adler's waist with everything she had in her. She wanted so badly for Adler to stay, but she knew she couldn't. There was a part of Adler that was a bit of a workaholic. Morgan appreciated that part. She loved that part. She was a workaholic herself. She knew her relationship with Reese had ended, at least in part, because she was too occupied at work; she missed the signs of their crumbling relationship. She'd always hoped she'd find someone who understood that this job – her family business – was her passion. It wasn't just her livelihood. In those dreams, though, the woman she was sharing them with lived in the same town.

"Okay. I have to go. My flight boards in five minutes," Adler said, wiping her eyes.

"Right," Morgan replied, doing the same. "Text me when you're in your seat?"

Adler nodded in response.

"And when you land?"

"I'll text you when I land. And I'll call you when I get home, okay?" She pulled Morgan in for a hug.

"Okay," Morgan replied. "I love you. I'll see you in a month."

"You'll see me on the screen tonight, when we FaceTime to say good night." Adler smiled a smile that did not meet her eyes. "I love you." She kissed Morgan's lips, wondering how she'd ever be able to survive without them for a month. Morgan's lips were intoxicating. "Drive safe, okay?"

"Fly safe."

Adler kissed her again. Then, she pulled away from Morgan's grasp, wiped her eyes again, turned, and headed to security.

"Addie?" Morgan yelled. Adler turned around. Morgan didn't say anything, though. She just stared at her for a moment. Just as Adler smiled and turned back around, she said, "I love you."

"I know. I love you." She blew Morgan a kiss.

***

"I'm so glad you're home." Paxton hugged her sister. "I've been kind of bored without you."

"No, you haven't," Adler replied and pulled away from the hug. "You've been totally fine without me. I'm the one that's needed you recently. I think I'm a bad big sister."

"I'm pretty sure the point of having a sister is that we can rely on each other."

"This probably isn't the best place to talk, huh?" Adler looked around at the room filled with about eight women.

"This might actually be the perfect place. Every woman in this room has been through what you're going through now," Paxton explained, motioning around her apartment.

"All of them?" Adler's eyes widened as she glanced around.

"All gay ladies, yes."

"Still."

"I'm not saying you have to talk to them. I'm just saying this is a group that understands." Paxton took a drink of her beer.

"I'm a little late to the realization party, don't you think?" she asked, stealing Paxton's beer.

"Actually, two of the women here came out in their thirties." Paxton pointed over at the two women in the corner of the room that were flipping through something on one of their phones. Paxton also stole her beer back from her sister. "They came out together, technically. Been together for two years now."

"Really?"

"One's thirty-seven. The other is forty now," she replied. "It happens all the time, Adler. Some people, like me, knew right away. I consider myself lucky, though. Andrea, over there, came out when she was in her mid-twenties. Gretchen, her wife, didn't come out to her family until technically after they got married. Melissa and Maggie, over there, have been together since high school. That's pretty cool," she added with a point toward two women likely Paxton's age. "Everyone is different. That doesn't make what you're experiencing less special or less on time."

"But I'm not out, Pax. I don't even know how to do that," Adler replied, sitting on the bar stool in front of Paxton's kitchen.

"You don't have to do anything. We're not in college anymore. You don't have to worry about Mom and Dad walking in on you while you're home for summer vacation. You're an adult. You have a girlfriend. Just tell them that whenever you're ready."

"It's not that I'm not ready... I'm honestly not worried about Mom or Dad. They were fine with you. They wore rainbow shirts, for crying out loud."

"They sure did. Don't think that didn't embarrass the hell out of me at graduation," Paxton replied.

"I guess I'm more worried about myself. I've never had a girlfriend. I'm already the only female executive at work. That's hard enough. Now, I'm the female executive with a girlfriend? What happens if we want to get married one day?"

"Then, you'd be the female exec with a wife. What's so wrong with that?" Paxton asked, finishing her beer.

"Nothing. Nothing's wrong with it, Pax. I'm just processing. You know I do that a lot."

"And how exactly did you not know you were into women?" Paxton laughed. "Us, lesbians, we love our processing." She rolled her eyes. "I had a girlfriend once that had to have a deep conversation before, during, *and* after sex. It was fine the first couple of times. Then, it got ridiculous."

"During, too?"

"And not in a sexy way," Paxton said.

"Morgan talks in a sexy way," Adler replied wistfully.

"She does, does she?" Paxton asked with a smirk.

"It's never been this good for me, Paxton." Adler turned to look at her sister. "I don't know if that makes me gay, though. I've never looked at a woman the way I look at Morgan."

"Adler, no one cares." Paxton laughed. "No one cares if you're gay, straight – except for Morgan, bisexual, or anything else. I know I don't care. I just want my sister to be happy. If someone else gives you crap over it, tell them to shove it and focus on their crappy life."

Adler laughed and replied, "I never thought I'd love someone like this, Pax." She leaned back against the counter. "It's not just the normal things, either. There's something behind all that that I've never experienced before."

"And the sex is great, too," Paxton added with a wink.

"God, yes."

"Save that for your girlfriend, Adler."

CHAPTER 21

"I**T'S** hard," Adler said.

"I know," Morgan replied.

"No, Morgan. It's really hard. It's too hard."

"Addie, come on," Morgan insisted. "You can do this."

"I've never done this before. I don't know that I can," Adler said.

"It's almost been a month," Morgan replied softly. "We only have three more days to go."

"Then, let's just wait until I see you. You can do this for me."

"I want to hear you, Addie. I *need* to hear you," Morgan said. "I'm so close."

Morgan rubbed at her clit as she stared at the ceiling but pictured Adler's face between her legs. She missed her girlfriend like crazy. She missed Adler's skin, her touch, her taste, her smell. She missed everything about Adler. She knew they only had a few more days before she'd go visit her in Seattle, but they hadn't had a lot of time for one another since Adler left. They did what they could with the time they had, but they hadn't done this yet.

"My clit is too hard. It's ready to burst, but it's too sensitive."

"Adler Williams, I'm going to come picturing you between my legs, using that amazing tongue you have. I want to hear you come, too. Touch yourself, please," Morgan practically begged. "I know you want it."

"I do, baby. I want you," Adler said, and Morgan heard the ruffling of fabric next. "I miss you. I want you."

"Make yourself feel good, and I'll really take care of you on Friday," Morgan said as she rubbed her swollen flesh. "God, I can't wait to see you. I want your nipple in my mouth while I have my fingers inside you."

That was all it took. Adler came before Morgan could even get herself all the way there. Morgan came moments later as she listened to Adler's moans of pleasure. Neither of them said anything as they both attempted to catch their breath.

"I cannot believe you finally got me to do that," Adler said with a chuckle.

"Addie, I love you. I love your sounds. I needed that," Morgan replied. "I've missed you."

"I can't wait to see you," Adler replied. "In some ways, this has been the longest month of my life. In other ways, it's like it just breezed by."

"You mean work breezed by, but when you were at home by yourself, thinking about me, missing me, it took forever?" Morgan asked.

"Yes, I do mean that," Adler said.

"That's how it was for me, too. I'm glad the contractor is getting to work on the new store soon, and that I've gotten all my managers hired, but when I'm at home without you, Addie, I can't stop thinking about how much I miss you."

"Is it weird that I'm actually disappointed you're coming here?" Adler asked.

"Yes, it's weird. Didn't you just tell me how much you miss me?" Morgan sat up in bed.

"No, that's not what I meant," Adler replied with a light laugh. "I just meant that I miss Tahoe. I wouldn't mind coming there again."

"Yeah?"

"Yes. But you have to come here first, because my sister is going to kill me if we skip out on dinner Saturday night," Adler said.

"I want to meet her, too." Morgan leaned back against her pillows again.

"Soon, Morgan. Soon."

***

"You must be Morgan," Paxton said.

"Paxton, right?" Morgan asked, holding out her hand for Paxton to take while she balanced her backpack on the other shoulder. "Where's Addie?" she asked, looking around the airport baggage claim area for her girlfriend.

"She said she was texting you," Paxton said. "She had a last-minute meeting get thrown at her and asked me to come pick you up instead. She said she should be right behind us and will meet you at her place."

"Oh," Morgan replied, disappointed.

"I know. I'm a poor substitute for the girlfriend you haven't seen in a month."

"I'm sorry," Morgan said. "I just miss her. I practically ran off the plane to get out here to her."

"Then, let's get you over to the apartment. It'll take us about thirty minutes. She only lives ten minutes away from her office; maybe she'll even beat us there," Paxton suggested. "And if her car is there, I will not be going in with you. I can't imagine what your reunion will be like. I assume it will involve a lot of alone time tonight."

Morgan laughed. She decided she liked Adler's sister. They got stuck in traffic when they left the airport. Instead of thirty minutes, it took nearly an hour for them to reach Adler's thirteen-story apartment building. Morgan's heart was racing. It had been the longest hour of her life. She wasn't sure how she'd made it a full month, when that hour had been so painful. Adler had texted that she was on her way home about twenty minutes ago. Then, she'd texted that she was home about ten minutes later.

"I promise I will leave you two alone until I see you for dinner tomorrow night. It's nice to meet you," Paxton said. "And have fun."

Morgan smiled at her and said, "Thank you for picking me up. I really appreciate it."

"Go inside and make out with your girlfriend." Paxton gave her a smile and a light shove.

Morgan laughed a little before she exited the car,

opened the back door to pull out her carry on and backpack, and then waved as Paxton drove off. She turned and made her way toward Adler's building. She kind of hoped Adler would meet her outside since she hadn't been able to pick her up. She sighed as she walked into the lobby and hit the elevator button. She lowered her head at the thought that maybe Adler wasn't as excited to see her as she was to see Adler. The elevator door opened on Adler's floor, but Adler wasn't there to greet her. Morgan's smile grew smaller. She wheeled her bag out and down the hall, checking the numbers as she went looking for Adler's apartment. When she reached the door, she didn't know whether she should knock or just walk on in. It was probably unlocked, since Adler knew she was on her way. As she reached for the doorknob, she thought that would be rude. So, she knocked once. The door opened immediately. There was Adler Williams with a wide smile, bright eyes, a red rose, and wearing nothing as she held it out for Morgan to take.

"Addie, you—"

Adler, apparently, had waited long enough for Morgan to take the rose. She dropped it to the floor, pulled on Morgan's hand to get the woman and her belongings through the door, and closed it behind her. Morgan's backpack was tossed aside, as was her carry on. Her lips were on Adler's. Her hands were in Adler's hair. Adler pressed her to the door. She reached for Morgan's shirt. She lifted it up and off, leaving Morgan in her bra. Morgan unclasped it for her and tossed it aside, too.

They pressed together and gasped softly at the same time when their breasts touched. Morgan had her own fingers on her jeans, unbuttoning and unzipping them before Adler got the chance, but it was Adler who shoved them down her thighs and past her knees. It was Adler who yanked them off over her shoes before Morgan could even kick off her sneakers. It was Adler who tore at Morgan's underwear until they were on the floor of her apartment. It was Adler that took Morgan into her mouth while she had her pressed to the front door. It was Adler who slid two fingers inside Morgan just as Morgan climaxed the first time. It was Adler that gave Morgan three orgasms in a row before finally releasing her so she could return the favor.

"And here I was thinking you weren't all that excited to see me," Morgan said, lying on the sofa with Adler on top of her.

"I'm sorry. I really wanted to pick you up from the airport. I tried to get out of that meeting," Adler muttered tiredly against Morgan's chest.

"Your substitute chaperone was a surprise, but very nice."

"You're being awfully nice to your girlfriend who hadn't seen you in a month and wanted nothing more than to pick you up but had to go to a work meeting instead," Adler said.

"I hate to tell you this, babe, but there's going to be a time where you'll have to forgive me for missing something, too. I almost had to postpone my trip, remember?"

"Postponing your trip would have been unforgivable." Adler lifted herself up to look down at Morgan. She offered her girlfriend a playful wink. "I needed you today."

"Did I deliver?" Morgan asked with a smile.

"You definitely delivered. I kind of want you to deliver again," Adler replied, kissing Morgan's lips.

"You do, do you?" Morgan ran her hands along Adler's hot back.

"I don't know what it is about you. Maybe it's me. Maybe I've been wrong this whole time until I met you."

"What do you mean?" Morgan's hands stilled on Adler's lower back.

Adler lifted herself up to straddle Morgan's hips and replied, "I've never wanted sex with anyone as much as I want it with you. I crave it all the time. In Tahoe, we had sex pretty much constantly, and I still wanted more. I haven't been with you in a month. Every day, I wanted you to touch me. I just had two orgasms back to back, and I want more." Her hips rocked. Morgan wondered if Adler was even aware of it. "I want you all the time. I never want you to stop touching me."

"Why did you say you were wrong this whole time?" Morgan asked, holding on to Adler's hips, encouraging her to rock them.

"Because I've never been attracted to a man how I'm attracted to you. I see your face, and I think you're the most beautiful creature I've ever seen." Morgan nearly melted at that. "And then, I see your body." Adler grasped her breasts and squeezed as she continued to rock. "God, that body, Morgan. Your breasts are perfect. Your stomach is sculpted out of marble. I love your legs. I love how they're the perfect combination of strength and softness. That's you. You're the perfect combination of strong and soft." She rocked her hips harder, sliding a little higher up against Morgan's stomach, using her skin for the friction she craved. "Maybe I should have been with women all along." She gasped as Morgan moved her hips faster against her skin, feeling Adler's wetness coat her stomach. "Or, maybe I should have just been with one woman all along." Adler stared down into Morgan's eyes.

"I love you," Morgan said.

Adler's hands moved from Morgan's breasts. She lowered herself down as she rocked faster and harder. Her hands ended up on either side of Morgan's head. She came on a hard thrust against Morgan's stomach. Before her last tremor had even subsided, she pulled Morgan's hand from her own hip and moved it between her legs. Morgan knew what she needed then. She slid into Adler. She watched as Adler rode her fingers. Morgan didn't do much. She somehow knew Adler would take what she wanted. There was something unquestioningly sexy about watching the woman above her come undone again at her own fingers. When Adler came down, she collapsed on top of Morgan once more. Morgan held on to her, wrapping her arms tightly around the woman she'd fallen so hard for.

"I love you, too, by the way." Adler kissed Morgan's neck after saying the words softly against her skin.

"Sleep, Addie. I'll wake you in a bit, and we can have a late dinner."

Adler didn't reply. She kissed Morgan's neck once more. Then, her breathing slowed and evened out.

CHAPTER 22

ADLER knew they were late; Paxton would be waiting for them. She'd never hear the end of it. There would be no lying. Pax would know what they'd been up to and why they were late to the dinner Adler had planned. Adler would take whatever Paxton would throw at her, though, because Morgan was on all fours in front of her on her bed. Her girlfriend's legs were spread. Adler's fingers were moving inside her. Morgan came when Adler dove deeper; her head pressed down into the pillow as she grunted out her orgasm.

"Okay. That is the last one. We have to go," Morgan said after she turned her head to the side. "I need to shower. You need to stay clothed and out here." She rolled over and pointed at Adler, who was still kneeling on her bed. "Did you hear that? You stay here."

Adler laughed and replied, "I'll stay here. You go shower."

"We're lucky I'm not a high-maintenance woman who takes an hour to get ready. Your sister is going to kill us." Morgan climbed off the bed a little wobbly before running into the bathroom to shower.

"Pax will forgive me. She knows how hot you are. If anyone understands, it will be my gay sister."

They'd spent much of the day in bed, getting reacquainted with one another's bodies and sounds. They'd stopped only to have a meal or a snack when needed and once to book Adler's flight the following month to Tahoe. That was a bittersweet moment. Adler liked having that ticket confirmed, because it meant she'd be traveling to see Morgan. She hated having to do it, though, because it meant she wouldn't see Morgan until then. Morgan had to fly back tomorrow. With how busy the expansion of her business was these days, she could only afford the weekend away in Seattle.

They'd gotten ready for dinner about twenty minutes ago. Then, Adler caught sight of Morgan's back muscles as she'd attempted to put on her shirt. That was all it took. Adler had to have her again. She'd kissed her way around Morgan's neck and shoulders, removed her shirt and bra, and had her on the bed within only a couple of minutes. Morgan had fallen on her stomach. Adler had kept her there, sliding off her jeans and panties, spreading Morgan's legs, and taking her from behind with her fingers.

Adler waited for Morgan to take her second shower of the day. This would be a faster one, of course. She likely only needed to clean up after what Adler had just done to her. The thought of Morgan in the shower, though, had Adler thinking about sex again. She'd turned into a horny teenage boy recently. She'd never thought about any of the men she'd been with when they'd taken after-sex showers. Her brain had typically moved on to the tasks she needed to do either around the house or at work. With Morgan, she could only think about the next time they'd be together. Adler wondered, as she walked into her guest bathroom to wash her hands, if that would ever change. It was likely heightened since they were in a long-distance relationship. But if just the thought of Morgan being naked did things to her that had her clit pulsing between her legs, would that change if they lived in the same city?

"I know. We're late," Adler said as she picked up the phone.

"Yes, you are. I'm at the restaurant already. Are you on your way?" Paxton asked.

"Morgan's in the shower. We should be leaving in about ten minutes," Adler replied, wiping her hands on the guest towels.

"Sex all day, Adler? You couldn't stop, like, an hour ago to get here on time?" Paxton asked.

"You've seen my girlfriend. Could you?"

"This conversation just took a very strange turn," Paxton replied. "It's kind of weird: you, being into women now. I'm not used to having to answer questions like that." She laughed.

"But she is gorgeous, though," Adler said with a smile.

"Yes, she's a beautiful woman, Adler Williams. She hangs out with a bunch of other beautiful women, too, doesn't she? Any of them single?"

Adler laughed and said, "Not the ones I've met so far. Just to remind you, though: they do all live in South Lake Tahoe, Pax."

"Well, I'm assuming you will, too, one day. Which means I'll have to visit," Paxton replied.

"What makes you think she won't move here?" Adler asked, heading out to her living room to grab her purse off the sofa.

"I don't know her all that well, but she doesn't strike me as much of a city girl. Besides, her entire business is based on the outdoors, which is much easier to sell in Tahoe than it is here."

"There are plenty of outdoor stores in and around Seattle. Have you not seen the mountains outside your window?" Adler sat on the sofa. Then, she thought about what they'd done on the sofa the night before. She thought she should probably change her underwear again, but she'd just heard Morgan climb out of the shower and didn't want to delay them further. "Maybe she could expand here."

"She could… But she's based there, Adler."

"Why are we talking about this?" Adler asked and stood. "She just got out of the shower. We'll be there in about fifteen minutes. Can you order the wine and whatever appetizer you want?"

"I think you mean appetizers, *plural*. I'm getting several, because you're late and I'm starving. I'll see you soon," Paxton said and hung up.

"What was that all about?" Morgan asked as she entered the living room wearing her jeans and a bra. She then slid her shirt over her shoulders as she walked toward the sofa. "I heard outdoor stores."

"Just talking to Pax about you." Adler smiled. "She's already there and is probably going to put one of everything on the menu on my credit card." She watched as Morgan's head popped through her shirt. Morgan smiled at her. "Worth it."

***

"What do you think of Seattle?" Paxton asked.

"I haven't actually seen anything except for the airport and the drive from it to Addie's place," Morgan replied with a smile.

"Addie?" Paxton asked her sister.

"*She* gets to call me that; you don't." Adler pointed at Paxton before taking a drink of her wine.

"I don't get that. Why do you hate that nickname so much?" Morgan asked Adler.

"Can I tell her, please?" Paxton asked.

"I guess."

"There was this girl in school. She was a year above you, right?" she asked. Adler nodded at her sister. "Her name was Hazel. She lived in our neighborhood. She and Adler were best friends. I was the annoying younger sister. Hazel called her Addie. Even I was allowed to call her Addie back then."

"Okay. What happened?" Morgan asked, taking a bite of her chicken.

"Well, Hazel and Addie here had a falling out."

"Hazel said some things to our group of friends that were untrue." Adler turned to Morgan. "It really hurt back then."

"What did she say?" Morgan asked.

"That I tried to steal her boyfriend," Adler replied. "He wasn't technically her boyfriend. She had a crush on him. I called him *for* her because she was too chicken to do it. He asked me out instead."

"You said no, I assume."

"Of course, I said no. The next week at school, though, Hazel – who I thought was my best friend – had written 'Addie is a slut' all over every girls' bathroom door."

"What? That's pretty extreme."

"Not for teenage girls," Paxton said.

"I didn't care about the stupid name." Adler placed her arm over the back of Morgan's chair. "It was that she stopped talking to me. She also encouraged all our friends to do the same. Suddenly, I had no friends."

"Then, she moved the following year," Paxton added.

"I got my friends back after that, but she was gone. I didn't want to be called Addie anymore."

"Should I stop?" Morgan asked.

"No." Adler leaned over and kissed her cheek. "For some reason, I really like when *you* call me Addie."

"That's a hint that I'm still not allowed to call her that," Paxton said to Morgan.

"Correct." Adler finished off her steamed broccoli.

"Are you going to get to take in any of Seattle sights before your flight tomorrow?" Paxton asked, pushing her mostly empty plate away.

"My flight is at three." Morgan did the same with her plate.

"You can at least let her out of your bed long enough to go to the market or something," Paxton said, referring to the famed Pike Place Market.

"She'll be back," Adler replied, removing her arm from behind Morgan and placing it in her lap instead. "Plenty of time for that on another trip."

"No offense to Seattle, but I'd much rather spend my time here with you, anyway," Morgan replied, kissing her cheek.

Adler glanced at her sister, who was watching their exchange with a curious expression. Paxton lowered her eyes when she noticed Adler's on her. They wrapped their dinner with a shared dessert between the three of them. Then,

Morgan got up to use the bathroom before they left. Adler watched as Paxton watched Morgan walk away. Paxton turned back to Adler.

"Go ahead. I know you want to say something," Adler said.

"Adler, she's really into her family business and Tahoe. She talked about it for most of the dinner."

"You think she talks too much?" Adler asked.

"No. I don't mean it like that. I mean she loves what she does and where she does it," Paxton replied.

"I've noticed."

"You do, too," Paxton said.

"I do, yes. I see where you're going with this, Pax. We're still in a new relationship. I've only known her for a few months. We've been together for a little over one. It's not like I expect her to move here right away. She doesn't expect me to move there right away, either."

"I get that, but I'm not sure you guys are really talking about what happens next. I mean, you wouldn't stop talking about her before she got here. You only talk about work, Adler. Then, you wouldn't stop talking about your girlfriend. I like Morgan. I think she's great. She's clearly into you, and you're definitely into her. What's the next step, though? You missed her like crazy. I could tell that. When do you guys have the conversation?"

"About who's going to move where?" Adler asked as she watched Morgan emerge from the bathroom. "I don't know. I guess I was hoping we'd have a little more time before we had to start talking about that."

"Are you worried?" Paxton asked. "Is that why you don't want to bring it up now?"

Adler wondered as she watched Morgan head toward their table. She had a smile on her face. Adler returned it, but it didn't meet her eyes.

CHAPTER 23

MORGAN watched as the contractor moved around the empty space with his measuring tape. He was a man in his mid-forties, with sandy brown hair tucked under a green baseball cap that had his company logo on the front. He wore the same color polo shirt, khakis that were a little too tight, and a pair of brown work boots that were caked in mud. He was, somehow, the perfect combination of professional and not quite professional at all. Morgan watched as he narrowed his eyes at the wall before he turned around to look at her.

"You had this inspected before you bought it, right?" he asked.

"Of course," she replied.

He made his way toward her and said, "Did the inspector not tell you that this wall isn't exactly level with the floor? It appears, this wall was added later."

"I knew that part. But it looks level to me," she said.

"Well, it's not. It actually also kind of goes at a slight slant." He motioned his arm out from his side straight before he moved it about ten degrees to represent a slant.

"What does that mean for the build-out?" she asked.

"We can keep to the schedule, but I'd recommend we tear it down and build it right. It's not load-bearing. It wouldn't add too much time."

"How much money?" she asked with a lifted eyebrow.

He removed his hat, ran his hand through his hair, ruffling it slightly, and then replaced the hat.

"Well, I could work up a new number for you tomorrow. Not too much more, though."

Morgan knew that was a lie. She'd always worked with the same contractor in Tahoe. It was the one her family had used and trusted. This guy was new to her. And this Jackson Hole location might prove to be more trouble than it was worth.

"How about you get me the new estimate on the time and money part, and I'll make a decision then?" Morgan suggested.

"I can get it to you by the end of the week."

"It's Monday," she replied with a squint.

"I've got to talk to my materials guy and the foreman about how–"

"You already started and stopped this build-out once due to some sewage problem that required the city to come out and fix. But when they got here, they said it was fine," she said. "Now, you're about to start for real, and you've somehow found something new that's going to cost me time and money. Here's what I'm thinking." Morgan pulled out her phone. "I'm going to find the first contractor online that pops up and give them a call. If they can get here and get me an estimate and timeline that works for me, your services will no longer be required."

"It's busy season for us. We need a few days to–"

"Take your few days. You'll just be bidding all over again, because I'm finding someone else who can get me a new estimate today," she scrolled through her email on her phone, not looking for anything in particular. "Go talk to your materials guy and your foreman."

"I'll have a new estimate for you tomorrow morning. We can start the work on everything else by Thursday, and you can decide if you want us to take out the wall and re-build it."

"Sounds great," she replied, putting her phone back in her pocket and smiling at him.

He nodded to her and walked toward the door before opening it and leaving without another word. Morgan was tired. She was frustrated. She was also lonely. She had one more week before she'd get to see her girlfriend again. Adler would come to Tahoe, and they'd have exactly two days together. Then, she would go back to Seattle. Morgan would bounce between Tahoe and Jackson Hole. This project had gone much more slowly than she'd wanted and planned for. Because of that, she'd had less time for her friends, her family, and her girlfriend that she missed like crazy.

The contractor probably needed her to be here for the initial work. That would mean she'd have to stay through the weekend, though, and postpone seeing Adler. She hadn't suggested to Adler that she come to Jackson Hole instead, because the moment she did, she knew Adler would say yes. The problem with that was that Morgan would be working if she was here. She knew herself. She knew she couldn't stay away from the new store if she was in town. No matter how much she wanted to spend time with her girlfriend, Morgan knew if she was within driving distance of the store and work was being done, she'd want to be here. Instead, she'd go back to Tahoe on Thursday night. She'd ask them to work without her here and hope for the best. Morgan also knew that part of the reason why she was so irritable was because she hadn't been able to talk to Adler in two days. They'd said good night to one another and shared some texts, but that had been it. Adler had been at a company-sponsored weekend work retreat since Friday. She'd been in meetings and at events day and night. She'd been so tired at the end of the day, that she'd had no energy for a real conversation. Morgan understood. She was just as tired.

She went back to her hotel room and got to work. She checked her email, called a few managers to find out if everything was okay at the stores, placed a few orders with some vendors, and handled a customer complaint that had come in from the Truckee store. Then, she closed her laptop, putting it away for the night, and grabbed her belongings. She checked out of her hotel and made her way to her favorite place. She went to her competitor to pick up some supplies, paid the fee for the few nights she'd be at the campsite, and parked her car in the lot. She hiked the mile it took to get to the best view in the world, unpacked her supplies, put her tent together, and stared at the mountains. For some reason, though, the view didn't feel as good as it usually did to her. Morgan knew why.

***

Adler hated work retreats. She went to them because she had no choice. She was a leader in the organization and had to set an example. She was also required to be there by the company's current CEO, Bill Richard. Yes, his name was Bill Richard. It wasn't Richards or Richardson. He had two first names. She liked Bill enough. He was a competent CEO, not a bad leader, and a decent guy. He was also boring and monotone. His speech – that was meant to inspire, only caused most of the leadership team to yawn. Adler managed to keep her own yawn to herself. When they broke for dinner, she decided to skip the cocktail hour and return to her room. She'd have to go to the meal that came after, since it was their last night, but she needed an hour alone. For once, though, she didn't want to work in that alone time. She wanted to call her girlfriend, talk to her until the moment she had to leave, and then count the hours until she'd see Morgan in person.

When she got to her room, she quickly moved to the bed to lie down. She dialed Morgan's number, listened to the ringing, and waited for her to answer. After a few rings, she thought about hanging up, waiting a few minutes, and trying again. Instead, she waited. She needed to talk to her girlfriend. She missed her now more than ever. Work was still mostly going well. She had hope for that promotion as soon as Bill Richard was out of the picture. But she also realized that now, it wasn't everything. It wasn't the most important thing.

"Hey. I guess I missed you," she said into the phone after Morgan's voicemail message ended with a beep. "And I do miss you. I thought I'd catch you, since it's still early. I'm about to go to the last dinner of this retreat. I'll try you again when I get back, but my flight's early, so I'm probably not going to stay up late tonight." She sighed. "Morgan, I love you. I miss you. I can't wait to see you on Friday. If I don't get to say good night later, good night."

Adler hung up and sighed again to herself. Her phone buzzed. She thought, hopefully, that it was Morgan. But it was only Paxton, telling her she could pick her up from the airport tomorrow after all. Adler typed back her response. She texted Morgan that she loved her. Then, she made her way down to the hotel bar for the last cocktail hour she'd have to attend before she saw her girlfriend again.

***

"Her first trip back... Do you guys have anything planned?" Kinsley asked Morgan.

"Nothing specific," Morgan replied.

"Outside of the bedroom, you mean?" Riley asked her with a smirk on her face.

"It's not just about that. You guys know that, right?" Morgan replied defensively.

"Hey, we know." Kinsley took a sip of her drink.

"It's not just that we get to see one another once a month and all we want to do is have sex," Morgan said. "We do. Obviously, we want to have sex, and we do. We will this time, too. It's just not all about that."

"Morgan, I know. I'm sorry if I made it seem like–"

"No, Riley. It's fine." She let out a deep breath. "It's not you. I'm just on edge."

"She'll be here tomorrow," Kinsley said. "Isn't that a good thing?"

Morgan took a drink of her beer. Kinsley and Riley had been nice enough to pick her up from the airport. They'd decided to grab a drink together before they dropped Morgan at home. Morgan loved her friends, but she was starting to think it had been a bad idea to say yes to a drink when all she wanted to do was go home and fall into her bed. She felt like she had so much to do and no time to do it. She had to work tomorrow. Adler's flight was getting in at five in the afternoon. She needed to wrap up at the office by four to meet her at the airport. They'd decided to go out to dinner before heading back to Morgan's house, knowing they'd likely not make it out again during this trip. It wasn't just sex. Morgan had meant that. She and Adler had never just had sex. They'd made love every time they'd touched one another. She knew she wanted to spend every moment this weekend alone with her girlfriend, but she also wanted Adler to get to know her life in Tahoe.

She didn't just want them to always exist in the bubble of Morgan's house; specifically, her bedroom. She wanted Adler to get outside, like they'd done on her first trip before they'd started the physical part of their relationship. Morgan wanted her to spend more time with her friends. She wanted Adler to get to know them, to participate in the couples' nights, and to be involved in all aspects of Morgan's life. Somehow, despite having a serious girlfriend she loved, she was still alone.

"I can't wait to see her," Morgan replied. "I've hardly been able to talk to her in over a week. Either she's busy or too tired, or I am. More often than not, it's both of us."

"You knew this was going to be hard," Kinsley said.

"What choice did I have, though? I'm in love with her. I'd rather be with her even if we're far apart than not be with her at all, James." She pushed her half-finished beer away. "I'm sorry. I'm not good company tonight."

"You two just need to talk," Riley offered. "Tomorrow night, we're going to Donoto's. It's the best pizza in South Lake. We'll have some good food, some good drinks, and we'll all get to know Adler better. She'll get to know us better, too. It'll be fun, Morgan. You look like you could use a little fun. My guess is that your girlfriend could, too, if she's that busy."

"She definitely could," Morgan replied on Adler's behalf. "Her schedule has been crazy these past few weeks.

She's basically running the whole damn company. It has ten thousand employees altogether. I don't know how she does it."

"Who knows? Maybe your stores will keep growing in number, too. You could have ten thousand employees one day."

Morgan thought about that. Currently, with the number of stores they had, they had over one hundred employees. The Jackson Hole location was sizeable. They'd need to staff it with thirty to thirty-five employees including management, at least during the busy times of the year. That would put them at around two hundred employees all in. She had no idea how she'd ever manage five hundred at this rate. She knew there was still growth potential. She'd yet to explore further west or further east. There were major chains, of course, but few of them specialized in the types of gear her stores featured. They didn't sell basketballs or baseball equipment. They focused their entire business on outdoor gear for all seasons. She could see them growing into other mountain and ski towns. Denver was next on her list, along with Vail and other towns around the Rockies. She could go farther, though. She knew that. But she also knew she was tired. She couldn't keep going at this rate at work at the same time she was attempting a long-distance relationship with another workaholic. Something would have to give.

CHAPTER 24

"THANKS, Chris," Morgan said.

"Want to tell me how is it that you're on a first name basis with our waitress, Morgan?" Adler asked with a lifted eyebrow as their waitress walked away from their table.

"We've all been coming to Donoto's for years. Chris has worked here for nearly as long," Morgan replied with a laugh.

"And she's…"

"She's gay, yes. She and Kinsley went out once," Morgan answered.

That got Riley's attention as she glanced over at her girlfriend and asked, "Oh, really?"

"It was *one* date," Kinsley replied. "Like, eight years ago."

"It was right after Chris had moved here, right?" Morgan asked, taking a slice of the deep-dish pizza and placing it on Adler's plate.

"Something like that." Kinsley took a piece of pizza as well, placing it on Riley's plate.

"Don't think serving me pizza is going to get you out of this story," Riley said with a playful smile.

"Hi, I'm Kinsley. I had a major crush on you for years and years. You forgot you even knew I was gay. Remember that?" Kinsley held out her hand as if Riley was meeting her for the first time.

"Wait. What?" Adler laughed.

Morgan served herself a slice of pizza. Then, she filled Adler in on Kinsley and Riley's story. They interjected with their own perspectives every now and then, but mainly let Morgan tell the story, given she'd bore witness to the whole thing. Adler ate her pizza with one hand. Her other hand rested on Morgan's thigh. She hadn't been able to stop touching the woman since Morgan had met her at the airport. Morgan had been smiling so wide. She'd brought flowers again; except, this time, she'd brought a dozen red roses. They were currently in the back of Morgan's car, waiting to be placed in water.

Adler was enjoying spending this time with Morgan's friends. Kellan and Reese were supposed to make an appearance, but Kellan had a last-minute patient show up at her vet clinic. Reese had opted not to come without her. Adler found herself feeling the same way recently. Ever since she and Morgan had started their relationship, she'd wanted to take Morgan with her everywhere. She wished Morgan could go to some of the dinners she had to attend with colleagues, or even with Paxton. It would've been so nice to have her girlfriend on her arm. Instead, she'd go alone and tell Morgan about them later.

"Okay. I was able to score you all a free round," Chris said as she placed four beers in dark green bottles on their table. "And by score, I pretty much mean steal." She winked at them and sat down next to Kinsley on the other side of the booth.

"How did I not know you dated my girlfriend," Riley asked from Kinsley's other side.

"What?" Chris asked.

"I'm Adler, by the way." Adler gave her a small wave. In their haste to get settled and ordered, she'd failed to introduce herself. "Morgan's girlfriend."

"I know." Chris pointed at Morgan and laughed. "She came in, like, two weeks ago and wouldn't stop talking about you. She even showed me a few pictures on her phone. I think she's obsessed with you."

"I am not," Morgan defended with a laugh of her own.

"She is, but I like it. It works for us." Adler winked at

Morgan and squeezed her thigh, sliding her hand a little higher as she did.

"And to answer your question, Riley, we went on exactly one date and didn't even really finish it. We knew we had no chemistry and would be better as friends. Right Kinsley?"

"That's right," Kinsley answered. "Chris is awesome. But she's not meant for me." Kinsley smiled at Riley before she took a bite of her pizza.

"I should get back to work. Don't tell the boss about the beer." Chris stood.

"Secret's safe with us," Morgan commented. When Chris walked off, she added, "Her boss knows she does this, by the way. She's not actually stealing."

The foursome finished their pizza, drank their free beers, and decided to skip out on the famous cannoli. Adler didn't want dessert anyway. She only wanted two things. Unfortunately, those two things were in competition with one another. She wanted to have her girlfriend on top of her, beneath her, touching her, and being touched by her. She also wanted sleep. She wanted a lot of sleep. She'd had so much trouble sleeping lately. It had amazed her, because she'd never had a hard time sleeping. Since Morgan, though, she'd only had a good night's sleep when they were together.

***

"Addie?" Morgan asked.

"Yeah?"

"Please don't kill me," Morgan began. "But I am exhausted. Do you think we could maybe–"

"Just go to sleep tonight?" Adler finished for her.

"Yes," Morgan replied.

They'd just walked into the kitchen, dropping off some of Adler's things. Morgan put the flowers into a vase with some water. Then, she stared at her girlfriend. She could see the small circles under Adler's eyes. The woman was still so beautiful, but Morgan knew she wasn't sleeping all that well. They'd talked about it, but this was the first time she was seeing the effects of restless nights on her girlfriend.

"We haven't had sex in over a month," Adler said.

"I know. I want to, Addie." She took Adler's hand. "Don't think I didn't notice how your hand was moving tonight. I just know I'm tired, and you're tired. We could get some sleep tonight, wake up tomorrow rested, and–"

"Spend the rest of the weekend going to town on each other?" Adler asked with a lifted eyebrow.

"That sounds like a pretty amazing weekend to me," Morgan said.

"Can I shower first?"

"Of course, you can. Do you want me to join you?"

"No. If you join me, we'll never get to sleep." Adler kissed her cheek. "I'll be quick. Meet me in bed?"

"I'll be there." Morgan smiled at her.

Adler made her way up the stairs. Morgan decided to make them both some tea that would, hopefully, help them both sleep. She put the kettle on the stove, grabbed two tea bags and placed them into two empty mugs. She added honey to her own and nothing to Adler's, knowing she preferred her tea without any accoutrements. Once the kettle whistled at her, she filled both mugs. She then headed upstairs, placed one cup by Adler's side of the bed and one next to her own. She changed into her comfortable pajamas, which she hadn't worn with Adler before. Come to think of it, they hadn't really had cause for pajamas. They'd slept naked. They'd slept in borrowed T-shirts and underwear. They hadn't slept in the flannel pajamas Morgan currently wore. She covered her feet in her extra warm socks, feeling like they'd help her sleep. She slid under the blanket and opened the book she'd started to read on expanding a small to medium business to an empire.

Adler came out of the bathroom minutes later. They worked to ready for bed in silence. Morgan brushed her teeth after finishing her tea. Adler took a few sips and did the same. When Morgan opened her book again, she watched as Adler covered herself in a long-sleeved shirt and a pair of sweats. She then slid into bed and picked up her phone from the bedside table. Morgan had two competing emotions. She felt comfortable, safe even, with Adler lying beside her like this. It was as if they'd been together for years and this was their routine. She also felt a little scared, because they hadn't been together all that long. They should still prioritize sex over sleep, especially since they so rarely got to see one another.

Instead, Adler checked her work email on her phone. Morgan read the next chapter in her book. They hardly spoke. Then, Morgan closed the book. Adler clicked her phone to sleep. They turned off the lights, slid further under the blanket, and turned to one another to say their good nights. They also expressed their love, shared a quick kiss, and fell asleep.

***

It was the best sleep Adler had had in weeks. Of that she was certain. She was also certain she'd woken up to an empty bed and had no idea where her girlfriend was. When she'd first allowed the dim light of morning to creep into her subconscious, waking her slowly from the blissful sleep she'd had just by being in the same space as Morgan, she'd expected the woman to be beside her. She'd spent all of a minute trying to decide on her next move. To Adler, there were three options. The first was simply to snuggle into Morgan, to breathe her in, and maybe even fall back asleep. The second was to slide her hand between Morgan's legs to wake her up. The third option was to slide down Morgan's body, spread those legs, and taste her for the first time in a month.

Unfortunately, none of those options were options anymore. Morgan wasn't there. Adler rubbed her face with her hands before she stretched her limbs fully. She stood, made her way into the master bathroom, brushed her teeth, her hair, and pulled her hair up into a loose ponytail. She made her way toward the bedroom door. That was when she heard Morgan.

"Why is this so hard?" Morgan said. "It's not even that much work. We've built stores from the ground up before. All I need you to do is to follow the plans. It's a few extra walls for offices and storage. It's hardwood floors I've already picked out. It's a few coats of paint, and that's it."

Adler wasn't sure who she was talking to, but she could tell Morgan was upset.

"This store is a strategic location for us. If you and your team can't do it, I'm hiring someone else. In fact, I think I'll just do that. Screw all the time I've already put into this," Morgan continued.

Adler made her way toward the voice, which was coming from the kitchen. Morgan saw her when she entered. The woman was holding the phone to her ear. She gave Adler an apologetic expression and turned away.

"Your new estimate is thirty grand over what we agreed to. We both know every job goes over the initial estimate. So, that means I'm likely out another forty grand, at least."

"What's wrong?" Adler asked softly when she moved around the kitchen island, taking Morgan's hips with her hands and turning Morgan to face her.

"One second," Morgan said into the phone, pulled it from her ear, pressed mute, and met Adler's eyes. "I'm so sorry. The contractor called me with another problem I have to deal with. Did I wake you?"

"No, I woke on my own. What's wrong with the store?"

"The stupid contractor keeps finding something else he'll need to change or fix. I had the place inspected before I bought it. Everything was fine then. Now, it's suddenly going to cost way more than I can afford to spend just on this store. I'm supposed to be opening smaller, satellite stores all around the main hub. I need that money for those and the equipment for rental outposts."

"Can I talk to him?" Adler asked, nodding toward the phone.

"Addie, I'm sorry. This is getting in the way of our weekend. I can–"

"Can I?" Adler asked. "Just for a minute." She held out her hand.

"What are you going to say?"

"You'll see," Adler replied, winking. Morgan handed her the phone, which she immediately took off mute. "To whom am I speaking?" she asked into the phone.

"Miss. Burns?"

"No, this is her partner, Adler Williams. And you are?"

"Mike Estes, from Estes Construction."

"Mike, are you familiar with Whitford Construction Group?"

"Whitford? Yeah. Why?"

"I've done a lot of work with Whitford in the past. They've always done a great job. Most importantly, they've done so at a great price and delivered on time. Whitford is worldwide. They're able to go a lot lower on price than most local places. We went local instead, because we felt that was important to the community. You're our local guy, but you're letting us down, Mike." She smiled at Morgan, who appeared to be in awe of her. "So, here's what I'm going to do. I'm going to call my contact at Whitford and ask him to make the trip to Jackson Hole to take a look for me. Then, I'm going to ask him for an estimate on time and costs. I'll compare your price and schedule to his, and we'll go from there. Sound good?" Adler paused for just a moment and heard him start to say something. Then, she interrupted purposefully, "And my partner and I will be flying in this afternoon. We feel it's pretty important to be at the job site as often as possible, given that there are all these issues. Of course, if Whitford is able to deliver, we – most likely – won't have anything to worry about."

"I don't think that's necessary," Mike finally replied.

"Well, here's the thing, Mike: I do think it's necessary.

McBride Outfitters is up to seven locations. It'll be eight with Jackson Hole. We're taking this company national, Mike. We might need to just go with the type of contractors that can handle our kind of account."

"Here's what I can do," Mike began. "I'll take another look at the issues I've spotted. Maybe they're not as bad as I thought they were. If that's the case, that'll take care of the cost issue. I've got a couple of guys I can bring on for temp jobs. I wasn't going to do that with this one, but I think–"

"Yes, let's get them working." Adler watched her girl-friend's expression as Morgan furrowed her brow. "And get that estimate back down to where it was originally. I'll still call my contact at Whitford, just to make sure it's on their radar. My partner and I will wait to hear back from you, Mike."

She hung up the phone before Mike could say anything and passed it back to Morgan.

"Wow." Morgan placed the phone on the counter. "Just… Wow."

"I do that a lot at work."

"Whitford?" Morgan asked with a lifted eyebrow.

"Brad Whitford," Adler replied with a shrug.

"Your ex?" Morgan asked with a slightly louder and higher pitched voice.

"Yes, it's his family company. They're all over the place and well known in the industry. I just name-dropped to get what I wanted."

"Have you talked to Brad since–" Morgan turned around to face the kitchen island.

"No, Morgan." Adler's arms went around her waist from behind. "I haven't spoken to Brad since he left that night. I'm not really going to call him, either. He'd answer, and he would do me this favor, but I just said that so Mike would get his butt in gear. I will call him if you want me to, though."

"No," Morgan replied instantly.

Adler turned Morgan around in her arms and said,

"Morgan, I love you. There is nothing between Brad and me. I thought it would help. Mike is going to get the cost back down, and he'll get the work done on time. If he doesn't, you can let me know if you want me to ask Brad to have his company take a look, okay?"

"Okay." Morgan nodded solemnly. "God, this is not how I wanted to spend our only weekend together."

"Good thing the weekend isn't over yet," Adler replied and leaned in.

CHAPTER 25

"THIS was a great idea, Addie," Morgan said.

"It was?" Adler asked.

"I needed this," Morgan replied. "I needed you."

"You haven't had *me* yet," Adler said.

"I'll have you as soon as we get home," Morgan returned.

"We are all by ourselves in here. You know that, right?" Adler asked.

Morgan looked around the serene space. Adler was right. They were technically alone. The masseuses, that had given them a relaxing and soothing couple's massage, had both departed and told them to take their time getting dressed before they could then choose to go to their mud baths, the sauna, or the hot tubs. The day spa had been Adler's idea. Morgan was incredibly grateful. She was also incredibly grateful, though, because Adler had just dropped the sheet that had been covering her naked, glistening skin to the floor. Morgan was lying on her stomach. Her arms were under her head, which was turned in Adler's direction. Her own sheet was still around her waist, revealing her back that was covered in massage oil. She watched with big eyes as Adler took the few steps to her own massage table.

"Addie, we can't in here," Morgan said but rolled over onto her back all the same.

"Why not? They told us to take our time," Adler replied, pulling off Morgan's sheet. "And I haven't touched you in so long, Morgan."

"We really should have had sex before we left the house." Morgan held on to Adler's hips as the woman climbed up onto the table and straddled her. "Because I would have been able to resist you if we had, but I am at your mercy now."

"You would have been able to resist me?" Adler asked with a pout.

"Who am I kidding? I've never been able to resist you," Morgan said. "We're in public, though, Addie. They'll have another appointment in here in, like, ten minutes."

"Then, I guess we better get to it. It's a really good thing that just looking at you turns me on so much. We already have a head start."

Adler took Morgan's hand and slid it between her legs. Morgan felt Adler's desire for her coat her fingers. She closed her eyes at the feel of Adler's skin. She stroked Adler slowly at first, playing with her already swollen clit. Adler rocked against her; their skin was sliding around thanks to the massage oils mingling together, which brought slickness but also the scent of eucalyptus mixing with lavender. They'd each chosen their scents. The room had been filled with them since the massages began, but now, this was different. The calming effects of the lavender, mixed with the strong eucalyptus, coaxed them to wake from their hour of relaxation. It made Morgan want to go slow and fast simultaneously. So, she decided she would. Adler was beginning to rock faster. Morgan held on to her hip with her free hand. She slowed Adler's pace. Adler looked down at her. She was clearly frustrated, which caused Morgan to smirk. She stroked her girlfriend's clit harder. Adler tried to rock faster. Morgan held on to her. She stroked her two fingers against Adler's clit.

"Move slowly," Morgan said softly. "Rock slowly against me. Watching you will make me come, Addie."

Morgan knew it would. Adler's breasts were slowly moving above her. Her eyes watched as Adler moved back and forth, taking Morgan's fingers with her each time. Adler leaned down, kissed Morgan softly, and sat back up again. When she did, Morgan felt Adler's fingers between her folds.

"I'd rather you come this way, though," Adler said as she continued to rock, slowing even more.

Morgan licked her lips and slid her fingers down and

inside Adler. Adler opened for her with ease. She lifted herself up and dropped back down on Morgan's fingers. Morgan's thumb grazed her hard clit over and over. Adler's strokes were causing Morgan's own orgasm to grow. Her toes tingled. Her fingers gripped Adler's hip tighter as they, too, tingled with the anticipation of what was to come. Adler's fingers moved lower, dipped inside briefly, and returned to Morgan's clit.

"That's teasing," Morgan said.

"I'll deliver if you let me," Adler replied. "Then, it's not teasing." She smirked. "There. There. Yes," she gasped out. "There."

Morgan curled her fingers. Just as she did, Adler lowered herself and rocked harder, allowing Morgan's fingers to find the spot she craved.

"Addie, don't stop," Morgan said. "I'm almost there."

"I won't."

Morgan caught sight of Adler's arm working behind her own body, making Morgan come undone beneath her. It caused her to go over the edge first. Adler followed close behind. Morgan couldn't control her muscles as she came. Her hand thrust harder and deeper into Adler, causing Adler to call out her name. She kissed Morgan in an attempt to stop the sound. It didn't work.

"Addie, they'll–"

"God, yes!" Adler lifted herself up and rocked.

Morgan could only watch as Adler's breasts bounced, pulling Morgan into some kind of hypnotic trance. She wanted to come again. Adler's fingers had stopped moving, but they were still in place. Morgan lifted her hips as a hint, but Adler was too far gone to take it. Morgan lifted up and down, craving another moment of release. When Adler finally slowed above her, Morgan came again. It was a smaller orgasm this time, but it didn't matter. Watching her gorgeous girlfriend take what she wanted from her own body was more than enough pleasure for Morgan.

"Is everything–" a voice started when the door opened.

"Oh! Oh, God!" The door closed.

***

"So, you two got kicked out of the day spa?" Reese asked.

"We did. We definitely did," Morgan answered.

Reese and Kellan laughed wildly.

"What's so funny?" Chris asked as she sat down next to them in the booth at Donoto's.

"Morgan and her girlfriend got it on at some high-end day spa. They've been blackballed," Kellan replied, taking a bite of her breadstick.

"You two got it on in public?" Chris asked.

"What? No. Well, technically, but no one was in the room. We'd just had a couple's massage. It had been a while." Morgan rolled her eyes. "Addie is impossible to resist. That's especially true when she's walking toward me naked and all glowing because of that damn massage oil."

"So, you're blaming the massage oil for not being able to have some self-control?" Chris asked her.

"I'm blaming not having seen her or touched her in a month. We had less than forty-eight hours together and had too many things we needed to do in that time. We had to multitask," Morgan explained.

"So, wait." Chris turned more to her in the booth. "Did you actually, you know, finish? Did you get interrupted before you–"

"We weren't exactly done," Morgan answered with a shrug. "But yes, we finished. I finished twice. It was hot as hell." She chuckled. "And there are plenty of day spas in South Lake. We can always find another one."

"Remind us to never do a double date with you two at a spa," Reese said.

"Agreed," Kellan added. "Hey, we're getting hitched soon. Is your girlfriend going to be there? I know you said she hasn't committed yet."

"She has. She's just busy, so she might have to miss the rehearsal and fly in for the wedding and reception. She'd probably have to fly out the next day," Morgan replied.

"I wish I had a girlfriend who was ready and willing to get kicked out of a spa with me. Then, I'd at least have a date for your wedding," Chris said and stood. "Instead, I'll be bringing my brother. One of my other tables needs me. I'll be back." She walked off to get back to work.

"Are you and Adler okay? Sex in the spa aside… You've seemed different lately." Reese nodded toward Morgan.

"We're both very busy people."

"And?" Reese asked.

"And I can barely get her for forty-eight hours a month," Morgan replied. "We did agree that we need to talk more. We kept missing each other, or we were too tired to talk at night. But we both need to make more of an effort because we need that. We need to talk more if this is going to work."

"If?" Kellan asked.

"I didn't mean it like that." Morgan dipped her breadstick in the marinara sauce. "I just mean that five minutes to say good night and a few texts each day isn't enough. We try to FaceTime on the weekends, but that doesn't always happen. This past trip, we needed to sleep so much, we hardly did anything."

"Outside of getting kicked out of a spa for fucking each other in the massage room?" Reese suggested.

"Exactly," Morgan said with a smile. "Friday night, we just slept. Saturday, we went to the spa after we had to deal with a stupid contractor issue. Then, we went home and…" She paused. "Well, you know. After that, we talked for a while. We tried to plan our next few trips. Your wedding is coming up. I told her I wanted her there. She said she'd make it work. We fell asleep, woke up on Sunday, had breakfast, and then I had to get her to the airport for her flight. Her parents invited her and her sister to dinner, so she had to leave earlier than normal."

"Because of a family dinner?" Kellan asked.

"They had something important to tell them," Morgan said after swallowing the bite of breadstick. "Her mom's a teacher. She's retiring, I guess. That called for a family dinner that gave me fewer hours with my girlfriend."

"Do they know about you, though?" Reese asked.

"Yes. She told them about a month ago. They want to meet me the next time I'm in town."

"That's good," Kellan offered.

"She says they've been great about the whole thing."

"Then, why don't you seem happier?" Reese asked.

"Because having her parents like me is low on my worry list. I have to wait five more weeks to see my girlfriend, and that's because I'm going to Jackson Hole for the next two weeks. She's traveling the next two for work. Then, it's your wedding." Morgan paused and sighed. "After that, I don't know. We haven't planned that far ahead. I just don't want a relationship that's all about scheduling time together. I mean, I know it's my fault, too. We're both working really hard right now. I love that she understands this part of me in a way..." She looked at Reese.

"That I never did?" Reese finished for her.

"It's not your fault. Obviously, you and I weren't meant to be. You're marrying this one." Morgan pointed at Kellan. "And I love both of you. I just feel like Adler gets that part of me because she has the same part in herself. I don't have to make excuses for missing a phone call or not being as available."

"Like you had to with me. I know. I get it. I was a bad girlfriend to you." Reese held up both hands.

"You weren't a bad girlfriend, Reese." Morgan glanced at Kellan and then back at Reese. "You just weren't the one I was supposed to have."

"And Adler is?" Kellan asked.

"I feel like she might be. I know I love her. I don't know much else, but I do know that."

"Then, you two will find a way to make it work," Reese said.

"And until we do?"

"It's not an until kind of thing," Reese replied. "It's not like you're in this in-between right now and, one day, you'll know the answer and you'll be in the relationship then, Mo. You're already in it. You're figuring it out every day. One day, things with the distance will get better. Then, something else will be a problem. Maybe she doesn't put the cap on the toothpaste, or maybe it's something bigger than that. You'll make it through that, and something else will pop up. But that's life. That's any relationship. What makes it different, though, is sharing those ups and downs with the one person you're supposed to share them with. If Adler's it for you, then I know you will work through this tough spot and all the ones that come after it."

"She's very wise," Kellan said, pointing at Reese. "It's why I'm marrying her."

Morgan's phone rang. She pulled it from her purse and glanced at the screen.

"It's her. Give me a minute?" she asked but didn't wait for an answer as she stood and headed to the door. "Hey, babe."

"Where are you? It's loud."

"I'm out with Kellan and Reese. I'm going outside. One second." Morgan pushed the door open and made her way to the sidewalk. "Are you okay?"

"No, I'm not okay. The thing I've been working toward my entire career was just snatched away," Adler said angrily.

"What? What are you talking about?" Morgan walked toward the end of the relatively quiet block.

"Bill is retiring." Adler sighed loudly. "I thought I was next in line. That's usually what happens. Usually, when the CEO retires, it's the COO or at least someone else in the C-suite getting the call-up. But not this time."

"Addie, slow down. What's going on?"

"Bill and the board are bringing someone in from the outside to replace him when he retires, which – I guess – is next month, because he wants to retire when he's young enough to travel."

"Okay. And you didn't get the job?"

"Morgan, pay attention," Adler replied immediately.

"Hey, don't get upset with me. I'm trying to understand what you're saying, Addie."

"I know. I'm sorry." Adler sighed again, more softly this time. "I'm so sorry. I shouldn't have snapped at you. I just got the news from Bill, and I needed to talk to someone."

"Okay. I'm your someone, Addie. Just talk to me." Morgan leaned against the lamp post.

"Bill decided to bring in someone with experience from one of our biggest competitors. She's been a COO for longer than I have. And she, obviously, has some insider knowledge that, apparently, she's willing to share with us as long as it doesn't violate the terms of her old contract with them." Adler paused. "I can't even be upset, because they're bringing in a woman. It's not like Bill's bringing in another white male to do the job because he doesn't think a woman can. He has actually hired a competent, experienced woman. I've met her before. I actually really like her."

"You just wanted the job," Morgan said.

"It was mine for the taking, Morgan. I was supposed to be next in line. I've worked my entire career for this." She paused. "I didn't see this coming at all. I've been waiting for Bill to pull me into his office to tell me he's retiring and that he's tapping me to take his place. Everyone has been waiting for the same thing. No one is as shocked as I am, but they're all still surprised."

"I'm sorry, Addie."

"I don't know what to do now. What do I do?"

"What do you want to do?"

"I don't know. That's the problem, Morgan."

"Well, do you want to quit?"

"Quit? No, why would I quit?" Adler snapped.

"Then, do you want to stay there and work for this woman?"

"I don't know. Maybe."

"I think the news is still fresh. Where are you?"

"At home."

"Why don't you call Pax and see if she can come over?"

"I don't want to call my sister, Morgan. I called you," Adler said, but it wasn't coldly.

Morgan could almost hear the tears welling up in Adler's eyes.

"I called you because I want to cry on your shoulder. I want to yell, and scream, and just have you listen. I want you to hold me until I fall asleep. Then, I want to wake up and apologize for all that crying, yelling, and screaming, and tell you that you're allowed to do the same thing to me whenever you need to and that I'll do the dishes for a month to make up for it."

"You wouldn't have to make up for it, Addie. We're in a relationship. I'm the person you should be able to do those things with," Morgan replied, wiping a rogue tear away from her own cheek.

"I just wish you were here."

"I know. I wish you were here, too."

"What do I do, Morgan?"

"I wish I could tell you the exact right answer, babe. I do. I just think it's something you have to figure out for yourself. I'm here, though. I'm here for whatever you need."

"That's the problem, though. You're not. You're *there*. I'm here. I miss you. It's been four days, and I miss you."

"I miss you, too. But I don't know what to do about it, Addie."

Adler sighed once more and said, "Neither do I."

CHAPTER 26

WHEN they hung up, Adler felt terrible. She'd ruined Morgan's fun night out with her friends because she hadn't been able to handle bad news on her own. Truthfully, she wanted nothing more than to curl up into a ball and cry her eyes out for the thing she'd worked so hard for and lost. She couldn't, though. She couldn't cry for that. Not just because that wasn't tough or strong or even remotely professional, but because she needed to cry for something else entirely. She needed to cry because she missed her girlfriend.

Adler had cried. Then, she'd fallen asleep and missed Morgan's calls and texts. When she'd woken the next morning, she'd dressed for work. She was glad it was at least Friday. She would go into the office, take her calls and meetings, send and reply to emails, and then, she'd go home early. Instead of staying until six or seven, she'd leave at five, like everyone else. She wouldn't make a habit of that. She didn't want people to think she was phoning it in just because she didn't get the promotion she'd been planning on. Her team and the company deserved better than that. She would allow herself this day, though. She could have this one day to just put in a normal amount of effort. Then, she'd go home, have some wine and popcorn, and go to bed early.

"Adler, can I talk to you for a moment?" Bill asked from her doorway.

"Sure, Bill." She understood that he wasn't really asking. "I have a meeting in about five minutes, though."

"That's okay. This won't take long." He sat in one of her guest chairs. "You've had a little time since you got the news. I wanted to check in."

"Check in?" she questioned.

"Adler, it's no secret that you wanted my job when I left."

"Because you've been grooming me for it for years, Bill."

"I know. I want you to know that while this wasn't my decision entirely, I will own my part in putting Danielle into the big chair," he said. "She's the right person for the job, Adler. Your time will come."

"When?" she asked, though not defensively.

"Danielle is fifty-two. She's looking for a place to retire one day. I suspect this is it."

"So, in about thirteen years?"

"You know as well as I do that CEOs of companies this large don't often last more than two years in one place."

"And I'm next?" she asked. "I wait two more years and hope that Danielle picks me?"

"You are amazing at your job, Adler. Everyone knows that. Danielle has nearly twenty more years of experience than you do. She's also worked for one of our biggest competitors. The board couldn't pass that up, and I agree. It's the best decision for the business. But when she retires, or if she leaves, we all agree you're next in line."

"I understand it's a business decision, Bill. I get that. It still stings a little."

"I know." He nodded. "I'm going to make sure Danielle knows you're her right-hand woman."

"I guess that's the best I can hope for now," Adler replied.

"And listen, I know you have a meeting. But if you decide you want to start looking elsewhere, let me know." He said the words softly, despite them being alone in her office. "I'll write you a glowing recommendation."

"Thanks, Bill."

Adler knew a recommendation from Bill would go a long way. She had no idea what a recommendation from Danielle would be worth, but a recommendation from both of them likely wouldn't hurt. She could work with Danielle for a bit to see how things go. If everything goes well, she could stay. She'd ride this little bump in her career road out.

She'd be named CEO in a few years at most, if Bill was right. Adler was a businesswoman. She was a professional. She couldn't argue with their decision, given the factors. She'd put this thing behind her. She'd work hard, put in a little more time, and then, she'd be rewarded.

***

"How's Jackson Hole?" Adler asked.

"Fine. But you're not here, so it could get better," Morgan replied. "I'm glad I get to see your face right now, though."

"Me too," Adler replied softly as she stared into Morgan's blue eyes through the laptop. "I do have to get some more work done, though."

"Addie, we've been talking for, like, five minutes," Morgan said.

"It's late, Morgan. You were supposed to FaceTime me, like, an hour ago," Adler argued.

"I know. That's my fault. The contractor needed me to look over something before he took off. It's finally going well here. I am sorry."

"I know. You apologized already," Adler said.

"It's late. Are you sure you need to work? We could talk more, maybe do something else, and then, we could both get some sleep," Morgan suggested.

"Are you trying to suggest we have phone sex right now, Morgan?"

"I wasn't *trying* to suggest anything. I suggested it. You can say no, Addie. God." Morgan looked away from the screen. "You know what? Never mind. I'm going to get some sleep. You get your work done and do the same. I'll call you tomorrow."

"Morgan, come on. I wasn't—" Adler leaned forward.

"No, it's fine. We just haven't done that in a while, and I miss you. But I get it. You're busy. I'm busy. I just miss you." Morgan looked at her with such love in her eyes.

"I miss you." Adler gulped back her sadness. "I'm trying to not show any hesitation at work, Morgan. I don't want people to think I'm not working as hard because I didn't get the job."

"But you already work so hard as it is. Just don't go too crazy, okay?"

"I'm not going too crazy. I'm reviewing spreadsheets. There's nothing less crazy than that," Adler replied.

"That's not what I meant, Adler."

"Then, what did you mean, Morgan?" she asked back.

"You already give that place so much of your time and energy. How much more can you give?"

"I thought of all people, you'd understand."

"Addie, I get working because you love it; because it's one of the things you enjoy most. I just don't get giving twenty-four hours of your day to a place that just passed you over for someone else. Every time we talk now, it's like you no longer even like what you're doing."

"That's not true. You're putting words in my mouth," Adler argued.

"I didn't put words in your mouth, Adler. I expressed my own. I stand by them, too. I have no problem with how much you work. I'm not Brad or any of your other exes. I don't even care that it takes you away from me sometimes if it means you're happy. I just haven't seen you happy in a while, Addie."

"Because you haven't seen me at all," Adler replied. "You're there, and I'm in Seattle."

"That's not my fault; in the same way it's not your fault, though. It's our circumstance." Morgan exhaled deeply. "Listen, we're both irritable right now. I'm tired. You're tired. Let's just have this fight another day, okay?"

"I don't want to fight at all, Morgan," Adler replied, suddenly realizing they were, indeed, fighting. "Morgan, I don't want to fight with you."

"Well, you are. We're fighting. It's not fun, and I don't like it, either. But I don't think there's any way around it. These days, it seems like all I do is say the wrong thing. I hate that. I don't want to walk on eggshells with you, Adler."

"Then, don't. I'm sorry. I'll stop bringing my work crap into our conversations, okay?" she pled.

"It doesn't work like that, though. You can't just not talk about something that's so important to you."

"I need to get out of this funk," Adler suggested. "It's losing the job that's got me acting like this. I just need–"

"More time? It's been two weeks since you found out, Addie. I admire you for sticking with it and making sure they know you're still in it at work, but you're working sixteen-hour days from what I can tell, and you're mean." Morgan paused, and Adler saw the gulp. "You've gotten mean. You're not a mean person, Adler."

"I know. I'm not. I'm sorry. I don't mean to be awful to you. I love you so much."

"I think maybe that's the problem. We both love each other so much that us not actually being in the same place to help the other through the shit we have to deal with, just makes us pick on the other person. I don't want to pick on you."

"And I don't want to pick on you."

"But our reality is what it is, Addie. I'm in Jackson Hole for the next week, and then I go home to South Lake. You're in Seattle, and then you're on the road for the next two weeks for work. It's going to be this way for the fore-seeable future, and I don't know how to fix it."

"Fix?" Adler asked softly, seeing the look of concern on Morgan's face.

"Yes, Addie. Something's broken here. Yesterday, I actually ignored two of your calls."

"You did?" Adler ran her hand through her hair. "Why?"

"Because I didn't want to talk to you," Morgan replied. "And I always want to talk to you."

"I didn't know that," Adler said.

"And I felt terrible doing it, because we never get a chance to talk these days. I felt bad for losing one."

"But you did it anyway?"

"Yes." Morgan shrugged one shoulder. Her eyes welled with tears. "I thought we could do this, but I don't know if we can. I don't know if I can, Adler."

"Morgan, don't say that. We're fine. We'll be fine. This is—"

"Adler, are you happy? Be honest. Are you?"

She thought for a moment and said, "No, but it's not because of you. At least it's not because of you in the way you might think."

"It's because you love me so much that us not being together-together is painful."

"Yes," Adler acknowledged. "I want to wake up next to you every day, Morgan. I don't want to have phone sex because I want real sex. I've never felt this strongly that I belong with someone than I do with you, now that I finally have that. I finally found you."

"And I'm here?" Morgan asked.

"Yes," Adler replied and wiped a few tears of her own. "I won't give up on this, Morgan. It's too important to me."

"Let's just take some time then, Addie." Morgan sniffled. "I'll think about things. You think about things. Maybe we can talk about everything – I don't know – in a week or something."

"A week?" Adler asked, holding on to the sides of the laptop as if it was Morgan's face. "You don't want to talk to me every day anymore?"

"Adler, I want to talk to you all the time. I told you that earlier. But something's got to give. This isn't working." Morgan pointed between the two of them. "You have some work things to figure out. I do, too, truthfully. We both have to think about what we really want from each other and what we're willing to give to get it. Because that's the problem… We can have it all. But we can't have it all like this."

"What do you mean?"

"I mean that we can both be successful career women. We can love each other and be in a relationship. But, right now, there are things we need to reconsider, because we're just irritated with everything and any time we talk, it comes out. I don't want a relationship like this, Addie. I want what we had when we first started dating."

"So do I," Adler agreed.

"Then, let's just take a breath. I'll focus on getting this store ready. You focus on work. We'll maybe talk next weekend just to check in."

"Morgan?"

"Yeah?" Morgan asked.

"Are you still my girlfriend?"

"Addie…"

"Morgan, it's a pretty important question."

"Let's just answer it next weekend, okay?" Morgan answered without really answering at the same time.

CHAPTER 27

"OH, Adler. How did you manage to get yourself into this situation?" Paxton asked her.

"I don't know. I went from being the happiest I've ever been to being the saddest within a few months," Adler replied, sipped her red wine, and placed the glass back on the coffee table.

"You knew about the distance thing going in, though," Paxton argued.

"Distance has never bothered me before. I used to actually want more of it."

"But, Adler, Morgan is the first real love you've ever had, right?"

"Yes," Adler answered and turned to her sister on the sofa.

"Then, what worked before isn't necessarily going to work now. You don't want distance with Morgan because this time, it's real. You want all of it with her."

"She didn't call me this weekend. She said we'd talk in a week. It's Sunday night. She's not calling," Adler replied.

"What's stopping you from calling her?"

"Nothing. She was the one that wanted the week. I didn't. I figured I should let her call me."

"She told you to take time to think, right?" Paxton asked.

"Yes."

"And did you?"

"Of course, I did. How could I not? She's been on my mind all week."

"And how has work been going with Bill retiring and this new woman starting?"

"Fine, I guess." She shrugged.

"You used to love your job, Adler. Did losing this promotion really make you hate it now?"

"I don't hate it. I love the work, I do. I'm one of those strange people that likes going to work to solve problems. I like sitting in meetings with smart people and talking about the next steps for the company. I don't mind checking email at night or working a little on the weekends."

"Where does that leave you, though?"

"What do you mean?" Adler reached for her wineglass but decided to focus on Paxton's reply instead, leaving it on the table.

"If you're doing all that work alone, because the woman you love is in a different city, does that still work for you? I know it did with Brad, and the others. But does it with Morgan?"

"I don't know," Adler replied with a sigh. She laid her head against the back of the sofa. "I don't want to have to choose between working hard – which is something I enjoy, and being with my girlfriend – who may be the love of my life."

"No one is saying you need to be a stay-at-home girlfriend, Adler." Paxton chuckled and turned to face the TV they'd left on mute when they'd started this serious conversation. "I think you need to figure out if your company is where you want to be. If it is, then you may end up losing the girl of your dreams. You have to decide if it's worth it. If you can find a way that you can still do long-distance, or get her to move here – I guess that works, too – you'd have to keep in mind that the distance thing won't get easier. It'll get harder. I've seen it happen. And if you ask her to move here and give up what she has there, she might resent you later."

"My options sound great," Adler replied sarcastically.

***

"It's nice to see you again, Adler," Danielle said as she shook Adler's hand.

"You too. Congratulations," Adler replied and realized

she meant it the moment she said it. "You're a great addition to the team."

"I appreciate that coming from you," Danielle said as she sat at the conference room table. "I know this could be awkward. Bill filled me in on everything."

"I promise, there's no awkwardness here. I'm happy you've joined us."

"Great," Danielle replied. "So, I know I don't officially start until next week, but I thought I'd come in for a few hours to try to get to know the rest of the leadership team and anyone else I might meet. I want people to know I'm here for them. That includes you, of course."

"I'm sure everyone will appreciate that."

"And Bill's retirement party is next weekend. I've been invited. I assume you'll be there," Danielle said.

Adler thought about it for a moment. She'd been traveling for the past couple of weeks. She'd barely had time to have Paxton over for dinner. As she tried to recall her calendar for the following weekend, she knew there was something she needed to attend. Then, it dawned on her: next weekend was Kellan and Reese's wedding. Adler had bought her ticket before she and Morgan had their fight. Morgan still hadn't called. Adler hadn't exactly called her though, either. Maybe Morgan was taking this time to think about what she wanted. Adler was definitely trying to do the same.

"Can I ask you a question?"

"Of course," Danielle replied, clasping her hands on the table as if preparing for an in-depth conversation.

"Why did you leave your last company?" Adler asked her.

"Oh, I guess I wasn't expecting that."

"What were you expecting?"

"I don't know. Something about whether or not I'll be making any changes right away, maybe."

"Will you?"

"How about we do one question at a time?" She laughed lightly. It was a pleasant laugh. Adler had to admit that she did like this woman. "I left my last company for two reasons. The first one is personal. My husband and I were having some problems. At my last company, things were always hectic. They're younger than this place. In many ways, they're still going through growing pains. I guess I was ready for less of that professionally – which is reason number two. It also helped my relationship, which takes us back to reason number one."

"He had a hard time with you working so much?" Adler asked and leaned in.

"You know, I used to think that. We had a lot of fights over it. But I think what it really was, had nothing to do with the number of hours I put in during the week. He just knew that while I was putting in all those hours, I wasn't happy doing it. It was like, the moment he recognized that I'd lost the love of my job, he tried to get me to recognize it, too. I wasn't ready then. We went through some tough times. Some nights, he was on the couch. Other nights, I was."

"But you're still together?" Adler asked, her heart thundering in her chest.

"We are. We've been married for thirty years. Our anniversary was just last month," Danielle answered. "Can I ask why you wanted to know?"

"I guess that's fair," Adler replied with a smile. "I, too, am a bit of a workaholic. I've always had to explain that to people I've dated like it's a bad thing. I've made excuses for missed phone calls, forgotten anniversaries, and dinners I've let go cold. I've met someone recently who understands, though. At first, things were great. We're in love. We're happy. We understand that we each have obligations."

"And now?" Danielle leaned back in her chair.

"Now, I don't even know if we're still together. We haven't talked in a while," Adler answered. "I don't know why I'm telling you all of this."

"Well, as someone who's been there – I'm happy to offer advice if I can."

"We're long-distance. That's the main problem. I'm in

love with someone who lives in another state and works just as hard as I do."

"And there's only so much time to go around?"

"Yes, but it's more than that," Adler said.

Danielle gave her a nod as if she should continue.

"I don't think I can really elaborate; you are my new boss."

"Not until next week." The woman smiled. "And I promise you, everything you say in here will stay in here. You have my word, Adler."

"I think there are two things, really." She inhaled and exhaled deeply. "The first one is that I've never met someone I wanted to miss work for. Does that make sense?"

"He's the first one you've wanted to call in sick for, right?" Danielle winked.

"She. She's the first person," Adler corrected.

"Oh." Danielle's smile didn't dim. "So, she's the first one you've ever wanted to call in sick for?"

"And sick, and sick, and sick," Adler replied, laughing. "I had a boyfriend when I met Morgan. We'd been together for a while. It took him months just to get me to go on a two-week vacation. When I finally agreed, I still worked. Then, I met her. I took two weeks off instantly and flew to where she lives."

"So, that's the first thing. What's the second?"

"I think she's noticed what your husband noticed about your last job," Adler replied hesitantly.

"Your heart's not in it anymore?" Danielle asked without judgment.

"I don't know. It was for the longest time. Then, I met Morgan. That's part of it. It's also that I lost this job I've worked really hard for. Please don't take that the wrong way."

"I won't. I understand. I've been passed over a few times."

"It just hit me like a ton of bricks. First, the loss of the job. Then, the loss of my girlfriend. Now, it's like I've lost the love of what I was doing all together. It's kind of seemed pointless recently."

"I've been there. It's the reason I'm here now," Danielle replied. "I take it, you're considering a career change?"

"Can I really talk to you about this?" Adler asked with a smile.

"Yes, you can." Danielle laughed. "I'm not interested in causing anyone problems. In fact, I'm interested in finding a home here, doing some good work, and retiring in a few years, just like Bill, so I can take that patient husband of mine on a trip to Ireland, which has been on his bucket list forever." She paused. "So, career change?"

"I don't know yet," Adler replied.

"You love this woman?"

"I do," Adler said, smiling at Danielle. "I wondered for a while if I'd ever meet anyone who'd put up with me. Then, she walks into my life, and suddenly, things make sense." She looked out the window, which showed the Seattle skyline. "And now, nothing does."

CHAPTER 28

MORGAN had picked up the phone a hundred times. She'd even hovered over Adler's name in her contacts. She'd never actually gone through with that call though. Instead, she'd wallowed. She'd gone to the store, done the paperwork, and made sure her employees had what they needed. She'd gone out with her friends a few times just for the distraction. She'd helped Reese and Kellan finalize everything for their wedding. She'd also cried. She'd cried a lot.

"There's a problem, Morgan."

"What's going on?" Morgan looked up at the South Lake Tahoe's store's assistant manager, Andrew.

"The plan you gave us to replace all the old backpacks with the new ones doesn't account for the ones I ordered last week. We have too much inventory and not enough room to store it all. I didn't realize we had that new brand's stuff coming in today," he replied.

"We can just store the excess in the back."

"We don't have any room back there. Have you been in storage lately? It's a mess. We still have the stock you ordered thinking Jackson Hole would be ready but diverted here when things got delayed."

"I forgot about that. Can you contact the shipping company and get that stuff over to Jackson on Monday? It's not ready yet, but the build-out is far enough along that we can store some things there. I'll let Holland know things will start to arrive," she answered and spoke of the new manager she'd hired for that location.

"I'll take care of it. But what do you want to do about the excess stock today?"

"You could always drive it over to the other locations," a voice came from behind Andrew. "Just an idea."

"Addie?" Morgan asked.

"Hey," Adler greeted when Andrew moved aside and allowed Morgan to see her.

"What are you doing here?" Morgan asked and stood up from behind her desk. "Andrew, can you–"

"I'll make the calls." Andrew left the office, leaving the two of them alone.

"The wedding is this weekend, isn't it?" Adler asked. "I probably should have called, but you never told me that my invitation was rescinded. I took a chance." She held out a red rose. "I got you this. I thought about getting a dozen, but I knew you'd be at work when I arrived."

Morgan moved around the desk. She took the flower from Adler's outstretched hand, feeling her own fingers graze Adler's and tingle as they did.

"I didn't think you'd come," Morgan replied. "I never called. You didn't, either."

"I thought it would be best for us to have that space to figure things out," Adler said.

"Did you figure things out?" Morgan asked. "Because I'm still kind of at a loss."

"Can we talk later? You're at work. I don't want to get in the way." Adler pointed out at the open store. "But, tonight, can we talk?"

"Addie, where are you staying?"

"Just meet me at six at your place. Can you do that?"

"You can stay. We can talk. Andrew can take–"

"I have some things I need to do. Six?" Adler smiled at her. "You're beautiful, Morgan Burns."

"So are you." Morgan smiled back.

"Tonight?"

"I'll be there."

"Okay. Can you stay in here for, like, five more minutes?"

"What? Why?" Morgan asked with a chuckle.

"I'll tell you later. I just need to…" Adler went to leave. She turned back and said, "Tonight at six at your place?"

"Addie, I said I would be there. I'll be there," Morgan answered with a smile.

"Okay. I'll see you then," Adler said as she turned and left the store.

***

Morgan couldn't focus for the rest of the day. She'd remained in her office as instructed. Then, she'd called Kinsley and asked her to meet her for lunch, because six in the evening was way too far off for Morgan to not have a distraction.

"She's back? That's great, right?" Kinsley asked.

"It was great to see her. That much I know. She's so pretty, James. Just, like, beautiful."

"You have heart-eyes right now. Is that what I look like when I look at Riley since she and I got together?" Kinsley asked, pointing at Morgan's eyes.

"You've been giving Riley heart-eyes since we were seniors and she was a doe-eyed freshman," Morgan replied. "Honestly, I give you a hard time about it, but I always kind of thought it was nice how you looked at her. I worried about you, given that she didn't seem to feel the same way back then. When she moved back here, she had a girlfriend she was planning to buy a house with. I worried then, too. Now, she does it right back to you. Heart-eyes all around in South Lake Tahoe, I guess. Reese and Kellan are about to put their heart-eyes on display in front of all their friends and family. You – with Riley. Even Remy and Ryan have heart-eyes for each other."

"And you have them for Adler," Kinsley said.

Morgan picked up her iced tea, which was all she'd been able to order. She was too nervous at what Adler might say or do later to eat food. Kinsley had ordered a sandwich and chips. She dove into her food without issue. Morgan was playing with her straw in an attempt to occupy her hands.

"I love her, James."

"I know," Kinsley replied. "Are you nervous about tonight? I mean, she did come here for Kellan and Reese's wedding. That means she's here for the whole weekend. It can't be bad news, right?"

"What if she came out of some sense of obligation? She agreed to be my date for the wedding. She flew in a little earlier than we'd originally planned just to tell me we're done officially. She'll stay for the wedding, and we don't have to tell my friends just yet, but it's over."

"Why would you even think like that? She brought you a red rose, right?"

"That could have been her polite way of saying goodbye," Morgan suggested.

"That would have been a cruel way to deliver a goodbye, don't you think? She just drops a red rose in your lap, asks to talk to you later with a smile on her face, then tells you it's over... She's not an evil person, Morgan. You know that because you love her."

"I've missed her so much, James. I wanted to call her every day, but I didn't know what to say. I've been going through the motions since the last time she and I talked."

"Yeah, we've all noticed," Kinsley replied. "We've been there, though, so we forgive you. I feel like each of us has gone through this. It might not be in the exact same way, but we all had to go through some stuff to get to the ones we loved. I guess it's just your turn there, Burns."

"I don't know what I'll do if it really is over, though." She looked down at the tiled floor of the restaurant. "I knew she was mine when I met her, Kinsley. I knew it. It was right. I'm supposed to be hers, and she's supposed to be mine. If it's that strong between us, why is it so hard?"

"It doesn't have to be. Just hear her out tonight. Maybe all the time she spent thinking about this was for the best. Maybe she's figured something out, and she's here to tell you all about it."

"And if she hasn't?" Morgan asked.

"You won't know until you talk to her." Kinsley paused and shrugged her shoulders. "And if she is here to end things officially, you still have us. You'll always have us, Morgan. We'll pick you back up until you find the one for you. Adler or no Adler, you'll always have us."

***

Morgan arrived home just before six. She normally wouldn't have stayed that late at the store, but she felt like she needed to get home just in time for whatever Adler was planning. She'd gotten a head start on their office supply order for all the stores, checked a few emails, and even called her parents just to keep herself occupied until it was time to make the quick drive home. She pulled her car into the driveway, noting another car was also there. She assumed it was Adler's rental. She pulled up next to it, in case Adler needed to make a quick escape after decimating Morgan's heart.

Adler was waiting with a bouquet of red roses on the front porch. Morgan took a deep breath and turned off her car. She opened the driver's door, grabbed her bag, and slid out of her seat. She walked slowly toward the woman she hoped was still her girlfriend. When she made it to the porch, she watched as Adler smiled widely and passed her the flowers.

"These are for you," she said.

"Thanks," Morgan replied, taking them in her free hand while holding her purse in the other. "Want to come inside?"

"Yes, but only for a minute. You need to put those in water. You also need to pack," Adler replied.

"Pack?"

"Come on." Adler pressed her hand to the small of Morgan's back. "Let's just get inside."

Morgan allowed herself to be pulled inside her own

home. She made it to the kitchen, where she watched Adler pull a vase from under the sink, fill it with water, and place the bouquet of gifted flowers into it. Morgan stood in front of the kitchen island, waiting for Adler to explain herself.

"Addie?"

"Okay." Adler placed her hands on the counter. "First thing's first. I owe you an apology."

"You don't–

"Morgan, please," Adler interrupted, but did so with such a caring expression on her face, Morgan didn't have a problem with it. "I am sorry. I let not getting the job, the distance, the missing you like crazy, and everything else get in the way of the most important thing."

"What's that?" Morgan dropped her purse on the island.

"I love you," Adler replied. "I love you so much, it burns inside of me." She clutched her hand to her chest. "The moment I met you, I knew, Morgan. I had no thought of ever being with a woman. I figured Brad and I would probably get married one day if he hadn't gotten sick of me. I never thought I'd find you. Then, I did. And it was amazing. Being with you is the most amazing experience of my life. I want you, Morgan. I only want *you* for as long as you'll have me."

"Addie–"

"Just one more thing, okay?" Adler held up her finger. "I don't want you to say anything right now. I was hoping you were free tonight, since tomorrow is the rehearsal dinner. Do you think you can go upstairs and pack a bag for the night?"

"Where are we going?"

"Just pack what you'd take if you were going to Jackson Hole for the weekend," Adler said.

"Am I going to Jackson Hole for the weekend? Because the wedding I'm in is here."

"No." Adler walked around the island and placed her hands on Morgan's hips. "Please, do this for me. I promise

I'll explain myself soon. It's important that you do it now, though, or we'll miss it."

"Babe, I–"

"It's a good thing that you're still calling me *babe*, but – please, Morgan. We need to go," Adler said.

"Okay. I'm in. Give me five minutes," Morgan replied, rushing off to the stairs, suddenly feeling so light that all the problems she had in the world couldn't touch her.

She grabbed her pack from the floor of her closet, tossed everything she thought she might need into it, picked up her hiking boots just in case, zipped the whole thing up, and rushed back down the stairs where Adler was waiting for her.

CHAPTER 29

ADLER wondered if Morgan knew where they were going once they hit the main road they'd driven on together. She wondered, but it also didn't really matter. Morgan would figure it out soon enough. It wasn't so much a surprise Adler was going for. She wanted the grand gesture. She only hoped it was grand enough and wouldn't be too late. She pulled the car into the lot, staring at the sky. She thought they had enough time, but they'd have to move quickly.

"Addie?"

"Come on, or we'll miss it," Adler said.

They climbed out of the car, grabbed their gear, and walked through the campsites where a few people smiled and waved. Adler headed right in the direction of the trail that would lead her to their destination. Morgan must have known by then, because Adler caught her smile. Then, Morgan took her hand. They entwined their fingers and walked hand in hand. When they made it to the water, Adler let go of Morgan's hand. She took Morgan's pack and her own, placed them on the ground, and took Morgan's hand again.

She walked them near the water where she sat down, pulling Morgan down to sit in front of her, between her legs. There, they sat in silence and watched the remainder of the sunset over the water. Morgan rested her head back against Adler's shoulder. Adler sometimes ran her hands over Morgan's skin and, other times, stilled them just to take in her warmth. Once the sun had disappeared entirely, Adler kissed Morgan's neck. Morgan understood what she wanted without words. She stood and pulled Adler up with her. They stared at one another for a few moments before Adler turned and moved back to their stuff. She couldn't get them a yurt this time, since she planned this little adventure so last minute.

Instead, they left the car in the lot and took their gear to the site she'd been able to secure.

They put the tent up mostly in comfortable silence. Morgan built them a small fire to cook a meal on and to provide a little warmth on a chilly night. They ate without talking about anything of consequence. When it got too cold, they locked everything away in the bear container and moved inside their tent. Adler lit the lantern, which gave them enough light to see by. They lay side by side, with Adler running her fingers over Morgan's face, through Morgan's hair, and over her lips. She kissed Morgan softly and chastely before she lifted up, rested her head on her own elbow, and stared down at Morgan.

"Here's what I'm thinking," Adler began. "I love you. You love me."

"I do," Morgan said, staring up at her.

"And we're miserable without each other," Adler added.

"I guess so," Morgan agreed.

"I can't just move here. You can't just pick up and move to Seattle."

"No, I can't."

"What if I gave you a reason to come to Seattle? Short-term, and you wouldn't have to move."

"What are you talking about?" Morgan wanted to sit up. Adler could tell, but she pressed her hand gently to Morgan's waist to keep her lying. She just looked too good in that position. "Addie, what–"

"I know why you got so frustrated with me before."

"You do?"

"You could tell I wasn't enjoying work anymore," Adler said.

"It didn't seem like it, no. After you found out you weren't going to be named CEO, things changed. I could tell."

"They did. But I think it happened even before that. I think it happened when I met you."

"I made you hate your job?" Morgan asked.

"No," Adler replied with a laugh. "You made me want something more than *just* my job. That something was you, and you weren't there. I wanted to go to work every day and come home to you, but I couldn't. That made work a lot less fun. I never needed that before."

"You need it now?" Morgan asked as she ran her hand through Adler's hair.

"I do, yes," Adler said. "I need you. I tried not to, when we weren't talking. I tried to plan the rest of my career, my life without you." She looked away from Morgan's pained stare for a moment before turning her own gray eyes back to Morgan's blue ones. "It was awful, Morgan. I'm not sure how I became a person who needs someone so much, but I do. I need you, but I also know that I need my work."

"I need mine, too," Morgan said. "So, I can't exactly fault you for it. I lost Reese in part because of how much time I spent with the business. You've lost boyfriends because you do the same thing."

"What if your work was my work?" Adler asked with a hopeful expression on her face.

"What do you mean exactly?" Morgan gave her a confused expression back.

"I may have scouted a few potential locations in the Seattle area for a *McBride Outfitters*," Adler revealed.

"You did what?" Morgan did sit up then. "You looked for–"

"Morgan, I want to quit my job. I don't want to be there anymore. If you say no to what I'm proposing, I'll just find another company, maybe be their COO or a VP. I'll even be a Director somewhere if I have to, but I know I don't want to stay where I am anymore. My heart's not in it."

"Okay. I'm listening."

"I'm not ready to pack up my life and move here, Morgan. I like living in Seattle. Pax is there. My parents are there. I was thinking... Maybe we could do some kind of a real trial run at the whole living in the same place thing, without all the pressure of one of us moving just to be with the other one."

"And what exactly does this little plan of yours entail?" Morgan asked.

"I was hoping you could continue expanding your empire in the great northwest."

"Oh, yeah? I'm a little busy with the mess that is the Jackson Hole location."

"And it'll be open soon. What are you doing after that?" Adler asked.

"I thought I might try to take a vacation with my girlfriend," Morgan replied with a smile.

"What if that girlfriend could work with you?"

"Work with me?"

"Morgan, I'm asking to join your company."

"Adler, I don't think we could afford you. You make twice as much as *I* do, and my employees make less than me."

"I don't care about money. I love you. I love that you love your family business. Morgan, one day I'm kind of hoping I'll be a part of your family."

Morgan smiled widely at that and replied, "What would you do?"

"Help you carry the load. You keep adding stores, which adds responsibility. I can help you scale effectively. I'm good at that kind of thing. I can help you with the new locations. I was thinking you could come to Seattle when the Jackson Hole location is open. We could spend our days checking out locations and deciding if it's the right place to expand the business. I've done some research already. Pax is a real estate agent. She's been helping."

"She has?"

"She wants me to be happy. You make me happy. This would make me happy."

"So, I just stay with you in Seattle while we find a place to put a store?"

"You can do most of what you do here remotely. Your

managers can take care of the rest. You and I can focus on the new store, or maybe even stores. We can come back here whenever you want."

"And what happens when we finish in Seattle, Addie? I live here."

"I know." Adler ran both hands through Morgan's hair. "With you there, we'll be able to do a lot of talking, Morgan. We'll have real time together. We'll work during the day and make love at night. We can plan our future together. We can decide together," she said.

"And you're not worried about what happens then?" Morgan asked.

"I am only worried about not being with you," Adler replied. "If I'm with you, I have to believe we'll figure the rest of this out."

"Okay. If I agree to this, you'll basically quit your job? You'll work with me at *McBride Outfitters*? Will you really be happy doing that? That's a big change, Addie. Like, a really big–"

"Morgan, can we talk about all the specifics later?" Adler interrupted. "I haven't touched you in so long. I miss you." She placed her own hand on Morgan's cheek. "I'm camping. I'm loving the experience. I loved it the last time we did it. I love it now because I'm with you. I'm doing this with the right person, and that makes all the difference."

"So, what you're really saying is that you're super horny because you haven't gotten laid in a while?" Morgan asked playfully.

"Yes, but I'm only horny for you. Does that make a difference?" Adler asked with a lifted eyebrow.

"All the difference in the world," Morgan replied.

She kissed Adler slowly. Her hands were on both of Adler's cheeks, holding Adler in place. Lips moved against lips. Tongues circled tongues. Then, Adler laid Morgan down on top of the open sleeping bag. She pulled off her own long-sleeved shirt, followed by her T-shirt and bra. She reached for Morgan's jeans, unbuttoned and unzipped them.

Morgan removed her own shirt and bra as she watched Adler half-stand in the tent. Adler pulled off her own pants and underwear. She pulled at Morgan's jeans and boy shorts until they were tossed to the side of the small space. When Adler went to climb back on top of her, Morgan rolled her over instead. She stared down at Adler with only love and certainty in her eyes now. She kissed Adler again.

Morgan reached down to tap Adler on the outside of her thigh to indicate that she should spread her legs. Adler complied. Morgan settled against her more fully then. She gasped as her center met Adler's. Both women were clearly more than ready for what was about to happen. Morgan rocked into Adler. It was slow and deliberate. Adler grasped her ass, encouraging her to rock harder and faster. Morgan didn't comply, though. She kissed Adler's neck, licked up to her ear lobe, sucked it into her mouth, and continued her slow movements.

Morgan's hand slid between Adler's legs. She stroked her just as slowly as she continued to rock into her. Adler's hips bucked up once and then twice. She was close. Morgan slid into her then. Adler came on fingers that were perfectly timed with Morgan's hips. She called Morgan's name, interrupting the sounds of the crickets and the water outside. Morgan slowed even further, despite Adler thinking there wasn't a way to go any slower. Then, she stopped, stared down at Adler, and smiled.

"I love you," Morgan said.

"I love you, too," Adler replied.

She rolled Morgan over to stare down at her beautiful girlfriend. This woman was the person she wanted to spend the rest of her life with. Adler had gone from being someone who worked all the time and considered her relationship – if she had one at all – to be a superfluous thing that accompanied her work. Now, as she looked into Morgan's eyes, she considered her job – whatever it may be in the future – superfluous to her relationship with this woman. They understood that part of one another. They both wanted to work. They wanted to make a difference in whatever job they did. They also wanted someone special to share their successes with, to talk about how to learn from their failures with, and to solve problems with.

Adler kissed Morgan slowly and deeply. Her thoughts about work drifted away. That was how she knew this was the right decision for her; not just for them, but for her. Only Morgan had been able to do this to her. Only Morgan had made her consider this life change. Only Morgan made that consideration a positive change that Adler wanted for herself. It wouldn't be done out of a sense of obligation to her partner. She'd be making these changes because she wanted to be happy. She and Morgan would spend more time together this way. Adler would still have the chance to do a job where she got to strategize and solve problems. She'd just get to do them with the woman she loved and the business her family had built from the ground up.

As she slid down Morgan's body to take her into her mouth, Adler's mind wiped completely. There was only Morgan's body, her scent, her sounds. For the first time, Adler was completely surrounded by the woman she loved, knowing they had these steps they'd take together, knowing they'd build a future together. And Morgan was right. That made all the difference in the world.

EPILOGUE

"Is the Seattle store ready?" Kinsley asked Morgan.

"Almost," Morgan replied. "I'm doing the final walk-through today. The soft opening is on Monday. Grand opening is a week later."

"And how's Adler?" Kinsley asked.

"She's adorable," Morgan replied, placing the phone between her shoulder and her cheek as she opened the door with one hand and carried her coffee in the other. "It's her first opening. She's going crazy making sure every detail is spot on. It's cute." Morgan laughed a little to herself.

"Are you being nice about it?"

"I'm only picking on her a little bit, but it's worth it. She gets all upset with me, scrunches her face, then realizes I'm only kidding, and other things happen," Morgan said with a smirk Kinsley could likely hear through the phone.

"When are you coming home, though? It's been, like, four months," Kinsley asked.

"Two weeks after the grand opening. I've got my flight booked. Stop worrying there, best friend. I'll be home soon." Morgan walked into the back office of the newest *McBride Outfitters*. "I have to go, though. Addie and I have a meeting."

"A meeting? Really?" Kinsley laughed.

"Yes, a real business meeting. We have a new payroll person just for the Washington store and, likely, all future Washington stores. We're going to walk her through every-thing."

"Well, that sounds boring," Kinsley replied. "I'll let you go. I can't wait to have my best friend back, though, Morgan."

"I know. I miss home, too. I'll be back soon."

They disconnected the call. Morgan and Adler had their meeting with their new payroll specialist. When it was time to go home, Morgan had a moment where she remembered she wasn't home. She was staying with Adler. They'd been sharing Adler's apartment since she'd decided that Adler's plan could work for them and for the business. It took a month to get the plan altogether. Her parents even met Adler, signed off on the whole thing, and then officially signed over the entire business to Morgan. Prior to that, they'd already given Morgan all the power, but they hadn't technically signed the paperwork saying as much. Once she revealed her and Adler's plan to add more stores, expand on the existing ones, and keep the focus on the great outdoors, her parents had signed their business away. They'd also signed off, so to speak, on Adler as Morgan's girlfriend.

Adler and Morgan had scouted locations together then. They'd decided on two, leased the first one, and started planning on the second one, which would require them to buy the land and the building on it. Adler worked on that more with Paxton while Morgan got the first location started. They'd worked well together so far. Sure, there had been some arguments. One had been a pretty big one. Morgan had actually slept on the sofa that night. Adler had gone out to the living room to apologize and pull her back into the bedroom.

"Are you ready to surprise your friends this weekend?" Adler asked later that night.

"It was so hard, not telling Kinsley. She thinks I'm skipping out on her party." Morgan straddled Adler's hips on Adler's sofa. "She and Riley got engaged. Like I'd ever miss that."

"Did she bring it up again today when you talked?" Adler asked, running her hands up and down Morgan's back.

"Not this time. She did text last night, though. I believe it was a frowny face emoji, a poop emoji, a few choice expletives, a devil emoji, and more poop." She smiled down at her girlfriend. "I love my job. But if that girl *actually* thinks I'd go to work instead of going to her engagement party, she's crazy. She pined after Riley for years and years, finally won her over, and then *Riley* proposed. I can't wait to see them, too," Morgan said. "I've missed them."

"You know what I've missed?" Adler asked, her hands sliding under Morgan's shirt.

"I know it cannot be sex, because we had some of that this morning before we went to work," Morgan replied, but her hips rocked all the same.

"I always miss sex with you. But that's not what I was going to say," Adler replied.

"What were you going to say?"

"I can't believe I'm actually about to utter this, but I think I miss camping," Adler said.

Morgan laughed and said, "Really?"

"I know things are busy right now, but… Maybe we could go back to Jackson Hole. We could visit the store if you want. But I was kind of hoping we could go back to that spot, spend the night under the stars, wake up, have some terrible instant coffee, and maybe go on a hike or two," Adler suggested.

"We could do that. Maybe next weekend?"

"Next weekend? Really? I thought I was going to have to convince you," Adler replied.

"Convince me to go camping with you? You're just as crazy as Kinsley, then." Morgan leaned down and kissed her. "Can we plan it later, though? I'm kind of busy."

***

Adler was glad to be back at Jackson Hole. She couldn't believe how much her life had changed since the last time she'd been here. That trip had been with Brad.

He'd surprised her. It had been a bad idea. She'd been terrible to him. She'd met the woman of her dreams on that trip. She was here again with that woman, and that woman was on top of her. She was sucking on her nipple. Her fingers were stroking Adler's clit. Adler was coming at her touch.

They'd made love under the stars that first night. Well, technically, they were in their tent, since having sex like that in the open was illegal. Plus, there was a family camping about twenty yards away. They didn't have the whole place to themselves that night, but their second night, no one else was in sight. They could hear the music of a soft guitar coming from behind them through the trees, and knew people were there, but they still felt alone. Morgan had her arms around Adler's waist from behind. They watched the beautiful sun as it set behind the mountains. Adler could not think of a better moment in her entire life.

She'd resigned from her job a week after she went to visit Morgan. Danielle had taken it well. She'd offered her a raise, less time at the office, and a few other things, but she knew Adler wouldn't take them. Adler had worked her two weeks before she said her goodbyes to everyone. A week after that, Morgan had flown to Seattle. They'd been living together ever since. Of course, Morgan always said she was *staying* with Adler whenever it came up. Technically, her girlfriend was right. It was Adler's place. Morgan was there temporarily. Adler knew they had some things they needed to talk about. They would talk, but not tonight.

After the sun disappeared, they retired to their tent. Morgan climbed on top of her. She pulled off her shirt and bra, revealing her breasts. Adler held them in her hands, loving the feel of them and the hard nipples she could see peeking through her hands. She lifted herself up to suck on one before sucking on the other. She then reached inside Morgan's pants, not wanting to wait for them to be off. She stroked Morgan through her underwear first. Then, she slid inside them, coating herself with Morgan's desire for her. She kept her mouth on Morgan's breasts as her own fingers worked inside, until Morgan came. Morgan rolled them over quickly. She smiled up at Adler, who knew what she wanted. Adler tugged at Morgan's pants and disrobed herself before climbing back on top of her.

"Tell me you love me, and I'll do it," Adler whispered into Morgan's ear.

"I'm pretty sure you'll do it even if I don't," Morgan replied. "But I love you."

Adler smiled, kissed Morgan's neck, and pulled back. She slid up Morgan's body and lowered herself over Morgan's mouth.

"I love you, too," Adler said. "Especially when you do this," she added.

***

When they woke up in the morning, they were naked and clinging to one another. Adler kissed Morgan's shoulder. Then, she left the tent to start a fire and make them breakfast. Morgan remained in the tent to start packing up their stuff. They had an early afternoon flight back to Seattle. After that, they'd have another few weeks together before Morgan was slated to return to Tahoe. Morgan had missed her home. She'd missed her friends. Kinsley had been so happy that Morgan had surprised her for her engagement party. Morgan had gotten caught up on everything. She'd slept in her own bed. Adler had been right there with her. They'd even started remodeling one of the bathrooms together. Well, Adler had helped her pick out a paint color and the new tile for the shower, but they'd talked about working on it together.

Adler's phone buzzed from its place on top of Adler's bag. Morgan didn't want to snoop, but Adler had given her the password. Adler had even let Morgan set the whole fingerprint recognition on her phone. She'd told Morgan she had no secrets from her. Morgan saw the email was from their contractor for the Seattle location. She used her fingerprint to head to Adler's inbox. She wanted to make sure it wasn't an emergency. She opened the email to find out it was only an update estimate with the new charges they'd been expecting. The contractor had sent a link to the form, which Morgan clicked on. The form opened in an internet browser. She reviewed the data, decided they could respond to it later with their approval, and went to close the browser. When she tried to do that, though, she accidentally tapped the bookmarks icon. That was when she saw them.

Adler had several work-related bookmarks. She also had a few non-work-related bookmarks. One was for a moving company. Another was a website with moving tips, tricks, and other things. The third was an article. Morgan clicked on it. It was called, *'Moving in with Your Significant Other: When's the Right Time to do it?'* Morgan read the first paragraph before she heard Adler approaching. She closed the browser, locked the phone, and tossed it on top of Adler's bag.

"Hey, breakfast is ready. I thought we could go for a quick hike before we leave. Do you think we have time?" Adler asked, sliding back inside the tent.

"Sure." Morgan smiled at her.

"And, I was thinking… Maybe we could talk while we hike."

"Talk?"

"You're only in Seattle for a few more weeks. We haven't talked about what happens when you go back to Tahoe."

"Oh, right." Morgan tried her best to hide her excitement.

"I had some thoughts. I thought we could walk and talk about them," Adler said.

"Walk and talk; sounds good." Morgan nodded.

Adler gave her a look of confusion and said, "You're being weird. Why are you being weird?"

"Not being weird," Morgan replied with a laugh. "I'm happy. This is just me happy."

"Then, you're weird when you're happy." Adler leaned

over and kissed her. "Oh, I was wondering if maybe Paxton could come to visit Tahoe. She's been asking me if she could stay with us. You – if she could stay with you. I would be there, too, obviously, but it would be at your house. *The* house," Adler rambled.

"Pax wants to visit all of a sudden?"

"I guess she wants to see what all the fuss is about," Adler replied with another kiss to Morgan's lips.

"Pax can stay with *us* whenever she would like," Morgan said with an emphasis on a particular word.

Adler caught that emphasis, kissed her again, and slid out of the tent.

"Breakfast, hike, airport. Let's go. We have work to get back to in Seattle."

"You're always trying to get me to work," Morgan replied in jest.

"You love it," Adler said.

Morgan climbed out of the tent. She watched as Adler took a moment to look out at the water and the mountains beyond. Morgan could only look at her. The view was perfect.

"You're right. I do."